About the Author

Ninety-year-old Etta Johnson is an author, teacher, artist,
matriarch of a large family and a World War II survivor.

Finding Home – Teddy's Immigration Stories

E. J.

Finding Home – Teddy's Immigration Stories

Olympia Publishers
London

www.olympiapublishers.com
OLYMPIA PAPERBACK EDITION

A CIP catalogue record for this title is
available from the British Library.

ISBN: 978-1-80439-231-7

This is a work of historical fiction.

First Published in 2023

Olympia Publishers
Tallis House
2 Tallis Street
London
EC4Y 0AB

Printed in Great Britain

Dedication

To my mama and papa's legacy and my dear sister, Trixi

INTRODUCTION

Today my immigration observations have come full circle, connecting past to present... World War II, to the end of the Afghan War. Full circle means that it's time to compile my numerous immigration observations into two books. Full circle... For the first immigration observations in this book (volume one) from Vienna to Vienna and the second immigration observations from Kabul to Vienna in the next book (volume two). Closing the circle from 1938 to 2021, includes all that I've observed and learned over the last eighty-four years.

Let me introduce myself – my name is Teddy Bear. I'm a fast learner and draw conclusions about what I observe. In other words, I quickly understand what's going on. I perceive parallels between historical events then and now. I document the enormous changes in technology, communication and transportation over time. I'm lucky to have a well-equipped modern office from which to write – describing events in chronological order, chapter by chapter, book by book.

You will time-travel with me to the last century to another continent, but you will recognize the same emotions that you have today. You will witness the Second World Wars events (in volume one) as well as the current world-wide pandemic and Afghanistan's fall (in volume two) through my eyes. You will experience two immigration stories close-up and personally. You will embark on an historical journey with me as you observe and draw conclusions with me. You will join me in gratitude for kindness and generosity of many people.

Background:

I am a real teddy bear and I was a fifth birthday gift to Steffi Dush from her grandmother. I lived with Steffi and her family – Papa (Tom Dush) and Mama (Mary Dush) and little sister Reggie – in German-speaking Vienna, Austria. I've been with Steffi ever since and now eight decades later we live in Vienna, Virginia. I observe and conclude about events as they occur.

CHAPTER 1

BIG CHANGES AT HOME IN VIENNA

<u>January 1938, Vienna, Austria</u>

Teddy observes: I sit on a sofa in a corner in the living room watching and listening as Papa and Mama, six-year-old Steffi and four-year old Reggie all look upset.

Steffi can't understand why she can't go to school like her friends. Papa explains, "Bad people are in control now. The new Nazi government says that people are not equal. They say that Jews or people with Jewish heritage don't have any rights."

"It's unfair!" Steffi yells. "I want to go to school like my friends."

Papa continues patiently, "You know our family is Christian, but your Grandmama and all your grandparents are Jewish. So, we are considered Jews."

But that doesn't help at all. "It's still unfair!" Steffi shouts angrily.

Mama tries to comfort Steffi, "We will have school right here at home."

Note: According to Nazi Germany's Nuremberg Laws (1933) – A person would be regarded as a racial Jew for purposes of the law if he had one Jewish parent or one Jewish grandparent, i.e. if the ancestor was 'of the Jewish faith'.

Teddy concludes: I began to understand the unfairness of discrimination based on religion or race.

March 12-13, 1938. *Anschluss,* war begins in Austria

Teddy observes: I watch and listen as frightening events occur.

In the morning, Mama and Papa listen to the news on the big cabinet radio.

"Hitler; the *Führer*, will now give an address about the *Anschluss* to the Austrian people."

Steffi can't understand what the man is saying, but she knows it is bad from watching Mama and Papa's reaction.

That night the airplanes' loud, awful sound wakes everyone. Mama and Papa rush their children downstairs to the cellar. Steffi holds Mama's hand and clutches Teddy tightly with the other, while Papa carries Reggie. They stay down in the dark cellar huddled close together for hours while the roar of the planes goes on and on. After praying, and singing together under a blanket, everyone feels a little better. Hours later, it is silent. The bombers mission is complete. Their threatening message to Austrians is clear – the Nazis are now in control.

Papa says, "We cannot live here under Nazi rule. We have to make a plan to leave."

Mama cries softly, "Now our homeland is gone! This is no longer our Austria, and I don't think we can live here! We can't raise our children here."

The next morning Steffi watches Papa as he reads the morning paper. The word *'Anschluss'* is printed in big letters in the headlines. "Papa, what is an-schluss?" Steffi sounds out the two-syllable word carefully.

"Anschluss," Papa replies. "It means annexing, joining together, joining our country, Austria, with Germany. Now

Germany and Austria are one country under one dictator: Hitler. That's why the airplanes came in the night to take over Austria. It's what Hitler talked about in his radio address yesterday."

"But you always told me we are Austrian," Steffi says. "We are not Germans. We just speak the same language."

"You are right, my child," Papa says, "We will always be Austrians in our hearts, whatever happens."

Teddy concludes: I understood that a dictator can take over a country unlawfully. I know how it feels to be frightened by real threats and anxious about the future.

April 10, 1938. Plebiscite – Austrians vote

Teddy observes: I listen to Mama and Papa talk about voting against the annexation of Austria by Germany.

On April tenth, Austrians voted in a plebiscite to determine whether they are for or against the *Anschluss* - to be part of Germany's Third Reich ruled by Hitler and his Nazi Party. The next day's newspapers announced that 98% of Austrians voted to approve *Anschluss*. Papa and Mama say the voting was rigged, that it was not a correct count of people's ballots. Austrians did not want to be part of Germany, but their votes were changed.

Teddy concludes: I understood that an election can be rigged.

Nov. 9-10,1938, *Kristallnacht; the* night of broken glass

Teddy observes: I watch with Steffi in Grandmama's apartment in downtown Vienna. Everyone is frightened at hearing glass breaking outside.

"They are smashing the store windows with hammers," Steffi calls, peeking out of the living room window. Within minutes the looters are inside, taking goods out and setting fire to the building.

"Where are the police, Grandmama?" Steffi asks. "They need to stop this."

Grandmama says sadly, "The police are Nazis too. They won't do anything to protect Jewish shops or people."

Steffi holding Teddy tightly feels safe in Grandmama's arms as they watch and wait. She feels comfort and kindness shining from Grandmama's and Teddy's eyes (Grandmama's fifth birthday gift).

Later when Papa comes to take Steffi home, he explains, "It was Nazi looters who broke shop windows and stole the goods from stores. They set fires to destroy stores and businesses that belong to Jews and the police did nothing. The Nazis want to take money and property away from Jews and send them out of the country."

Mama says, "I just heard on the radio that they are calling it *Kristallnacht*, the night of broken glass."

"This makes it even clearer that we have to leave," Papa says. "Since the *Anschluss*, I have been searching for ways to leave our country and find a home where we don't have to be afraid."

"And we have to be sure that Grandmama comes with us," Mama says.

Teddy concludes: I understood that it is impossible to live in a country which does not protect all of its citizens.

Christmas 1938

Teddy observes: I participated in the family's Christmas celebration despite the Nazi takeover of Austria.

On Christmas Eve, Mama leads Steffi and Reggie into the living room. Steffi looks with wonder at the candle-lit Christmas tree in the dark room. "Oh, it's so beautiful!"

Reggie claps her little hands in delight. Papa, Mama, Steffi and Reggie hold hands and dance around the tree. The little girls high-pitched voices blend with their parents as they sing, *Oh Tannenbaum* (Oh, Christmas tree). The angel on the very top of the tree glimmers in the candlelight.

On Christmas Day, the organ music echoes in the church with "*Stille nacht, heilige nacht*" (Silent night, holy night). Everyone joins in singing the traditional hymn celebrating the birth of the Christ child.

On December sixth the family celebrated Saint Nicholas Day as usual. St. Nicolas, the special children's saint brought Steffi and Reggie small gifts since they had been good all year. Steffi was relieved that the dreaded Krampus who put coal in naughty children's stockings did not appear.

Teddy concludes: I understood that it is important to maintain Christmas traditions.

April 20, 1939. Preparing to leave home

Teddy observes: As I watch Mama pack and listen to the conversation, I can feel Steffi's fear and anxiety.

Two suitcases, one for Steffi and one for Reggie are open on the bed. Mama packs clothes and checks them off on a required Clothing List for Children.

"We have to be ready, since you will leave on the *Kindertransport* in four days," Mama says.

Steffi still can't quite believe it. "We're going on a trip

without you and Papa, just me and Reggie." Although they had said tearful good-byes to Grandmama over the weekend, it was hard to take in the changes occurring.

Papa had carefully explained their decision, "We are sending you both to England where you will be safe from the Nazis. You know that Hitler and the Nazis are hurting Jews and people with Jewish heritage like us."

Kindertransport officials had interviewed Papa and Mama, completed documents and received permission for Steffi and Reggie to join the *Kindertransport* from Vienna to England. No parents could go, only children. A Quaker lady would take care of the children on the trip until they met their new family in England. The *Kindertransport* (children's transport) was sponsored by the Quakers are the Society of Friends.

Steffi looks at the picture postcard (sent by airmail) from England again and reads the message, "This is a picture of our English village. You will come and live with us here. It's signed by Dora and Aunt Alice."

"I'm so glad you will live with Dora and Aunt Alice in England," Mama says. "They will be your family until we can be together again."

Days ago, when Steffi got the postcard, she read the address aloud and finally understood the meaning of *Anschluss*. The address on the right side of the card under the British stamp said: *Steffi and Reggie Dush, 13 Alter Strasse, Vienna, Germany.*

"Mama, why does it say Vienna, Germany? Vienna is in Austria," Steffi had asked puzzled. "It should say Vienna, Austria."

"Austria became part of Germany with the *Anschluss*," Mama explained. "That is why we don't feel at home here and can't live here anymore.

Mama stops packing, looks at the clock and says, "It is time for you to get ready to go to the doctor." Another requirement: a physical exam by a doctor within forty-eight hours of departure. The doctor has to verify that each child is healthy.

Teddy concludes: I understood that a big change is scary, but it helps if you know where you are going and how.

Note: Eighty-two years later a medical exam and a negative COVID test are requirements for departure for new immigrants from Afghanistan to the U.S.

April 26, 1939. Leaving home

Teddy observes: I am in Steffi's backpack at the train station. I am sad to leave and anxious about the future as goodbyes are said.

Papa and Mama hold Steffi's and Reggie's hands tightly in the enormous Westbahnhof train station at nine o'clock at night. They don't have any luggage with them, since Papa was required to take it to the Jewish Center to be inspected. Papa says they might be inspected again when the train reaches the German border. Papa and Mama decide that it is best for Teddy to travel in Steffi's small, canvas backpack.

"There are so many people," Steffi says anxiously. "How will we ever find Miss Kraus?"

Miss Kraus is the lady who will accompany all the children from Vienna to London on this Children's Transport. Steffi and Reggie met her last week when they went to the Society of Friends office with Mama. Miss Kraus had given each child a card with a number on a string. She said it was an identification card that they would wear on their journey to England.

"Remember your guardian angel is always with you," Papa says in his good-bye.

Then Steffi is shaking and sobbing as she says good-bye to Mama and Papa. Reggie is speechlessly clinging to Papa.

"Don't be scared," Steff tries to comfort Reggie although she feels cold and more afraid than she's ever been in her life. Reggie didn't truly understand that she was leaving on the train without her parents until this very moment. The conductor lifts each child up the steps onto the train and Miss Krauss takes them to their seats. Other boys and girls are already seated, some with their faces pressed against the windows, crying.

Teddy concludes: I understood that when the train left the train station, we left behind everything we knew and loved and traveled into unknown territory.

CHAPTER 2

TRANSITION BETWEEN HOMES

April 26, 1939. On the train

Teddy observes: We fall asleep lulled by the clackety-clack of the steam train as it moves through the dark night.

Steffi wakes up startled as the train screeches to a stop amid glaring lights. For a second, she can't remember where she is and why Reggie is sleeping curled up against her.

"I think we're at the German border," Steffi whispers to Reggie. "Someone's getting on the train."

Three uniformed officials stomp into the coach full of startled children. They demand to see each child's identification card. Miss Kraus comes forward saying, "I am in charge of this *Kindertransport*. I will be glad to help, so the children won't be frightened."

The official says rudely, "We don't need your help, Miss Quaker. You are no real German. Go to your seat and leave us to do our job."

Miss Kraus tries to smile reassuringly at each of the children as she passes their seats, but everyone is now awake and frightened. Reggie's thumb is in her mouth and Steffi holds her other hand tightly. They watch without moving as the officials work their way down the car row by row.

Steffi is cold and trembling by the time the official gets to her row. But she bravely holds out her identification card to the frowning man. "This is my card," she says clearly. Then she hands him Reggie's card. "And here is my sister's card. She is only five."

The man examines the cards carefully back and front, checking them against a list. He thrusts the cards back at Steffi and says, "Show me your luggage."

"I only have this backpack," Steffi says, pointing to the backpack under her seat. "I do not know where our suitcases are."

"Open it up!" the official barks impatiently. "We inspect your suitcases in the baggage car."

The girls watch barely breathing as he rummages through the contents of the bag. Without another word, the officer throws the backpack in Steffi's lap and goes on to the next row.

Steffi breathes a big sigh of relief and whispers to Reggie, "It's alright! We're alright, but I was so scared when he picked up Teddy."

Miss Kraus announces quietly, "When we leave this station, we will be out of Germany and in the Netherlands, Holland."

Teddy concludes: I was very scared when the official pulled me out and dumped me back. I learned that you can be frightened, yet also brave.

Night on the ferry

Teddy observes: Now I am out of the backpack and with Steffi, I feel the steady motion of the large ferry boat moving swiftly across the water.

Miss Kraus helps Steffi, Reggie and all the *Kindertransport* children off the train at the Hook of Holland dock. There they immediately board the ferry, the Princess Beatrix. This big boat will carry them across the North Sea to Harwich on the east coast of England.

Steffi and Reggie share a small cabin with twelve-year-old Helga from Salzburg and ten-year-old Greta from Vienna. The two older girls, Greta and Helga immediately take possession of the bottom bunks, leaving the top bunks to the younger children.

"What's that bed doing up by the ceiling?" Reggie asks when they enter the small, low cabin assigned to the four girls for the short trip.

"Maybe we should ask Miss Kraus to put it on the floor?" Steffi says, as neither of the sisters had ever seen double-decker bunk beds before.

"You are a stupid, little kid if you don't know what bunk beds are," Helga jeers, sticking out her tongue at Steffi.

Steffi replies angrily, "Well, I bet you don't know everything in the world either."

When the ship suddenly lurches, the older girls are able to keep their footing. However, Reggie falls against one of the bunks hitting her forehead on the wooden frame. Helga immediately goes to help her up.

"Ow-ow!" Reggie yells holding her hand on her head. "That bad old sea made me fall over!" Instead of crying with pain, she is laughing and excited. Jumping around and yelling, "Do it again, sea, do it again!"

Steffi, Greta and Helga jump and yell with her, glad to have a little fun after the sadness of leaving home. When Helga sings, "Sailing, sailing, over the bounding main," the other girls join in, dancing around wildly. By the time Miss Kraus tells them to come to breakfast in the boat's dining room, the girls are giggling and have become friends.

Teddy concludes: I understood that being with other people and being able to find humor in a situation can help when you are sad and scared.

Arrival in England

Teddy observes: I hear the announcement on the ship's loudspeaker. When we get off the ship in England, I breathe the clean air of freedom and get a look at this new country.

"Prepare to disembark at twenty-four hours. The ship will dock at Harwich at twelve noon." The girls all cheer and get ready to leave the cabin.

Everyone follows Miss Kraus down the gangplank and off the ferry. "We are in England. Hooray! We are free!"

Miss Krauss leads us in some exercises right there on the dock. "Let's get the kinks out of our joints after our long journey." Then we walk into a waiting room nearby. "Your sponsors will meet you here."

"Now we'll see Dora and Aunt Alice," Steffi says to Reggie. "We'll meet our new family and go to our new home."

Teddy concludes: I understood that we were now in a new country where people are free and equal.

CHAPTER 3

AT HOME IN ENGLAND

April 1939. A new family and home in an English village

Teddy observes: I become acquainted with everyone and everything in our new home.

Everything is different... The house, the garden, the small village, the language, a dog. a lot of changes. Yet Dora and Aunt Alice's kindness make Steffi and Reggie feel cared for and secure.

Dora, a young lady with a kind smile, had met Steffi and Reggie in Harwich and drove them to her home. She spoke to them slowly in her limited German, knowing they didn't speak English. When they arrived at the house, Aunt Alice, a sweet older lady welcomed the children to her home and family. She showed them their new bedroom and the w.c (water closet) as she called the toilet. Best of all she introduced them to their dog, David, a friendly black-and-white Dalmatian. The girls had never had a live pet.

Dora tells the children that she sent a telegram to their Mama and Papa that they had arrived safely in their new home.

David accompanies them on a tour of the front garden and Steffi holds Teddy. A flowering pear tree casts shade over a table and four chairs on the green lawn. The flowerbeds under the hedge facing the road are neatly trimmed and a few late tulips are still blooming. In this colorful, peaceful garden, Steffi closes her eyes and wishes with all her might that her Mama and Papa would magically appear beside her. When tears start rolling down her cheeks Aunt Alice takes the homesick child in her arms. Seeing Steffi's distress, Reggie starts crying too, "Papa, Papa!" When Dora picks her up, she buries her head on Dora's shoulder, thumb in her mouth, and sobs softly in Dora's arms. Steffi and Reggie are homesick but feel loved and secure in their new home.

Teddy concludes: I understood that children to adapt to changes when they feel secure.

New experiences

Teddy observes: I watch, listen and learn about our new environment.

Dora takes the girls for daily walks in the village. She takes them to the village shop and to the river; they walk down lanes and climb over stiles. They see cows and sheep on the farms they pass and Dora introduces Steffi and Reggie to all her friends. On Sunday, they all go to the old stone Anglican church and listen to hymns they know but in English.

The children become accustomed to five o'clock high tea with small savory sandwiches, scones and milky tea. Steffi helps to feed the hens in the chicken coop and learns how to gather eggs. Both girls learn to pick ripe early peas growing on trellises in the large kitchen garden at the side of the house. Lots of new experiences, a whole different way of life to suburban Vienna.

They walk everywhere, as Dora and Aunt Alice, like other villagers, don't have a car. On the rare trips to the big city of Norwich five miles away they ride a local bus.

"Would you like to see a castle?" Dora asks one day.

"I visit Schöenbrun Castle in Vienna... Very old," Steffi replies.

"We can ride a bus and go to Norwich Castle," Dora says. "It is also very old."

On another day, Steffi says, "I write go *auf* sea." Steffi wants to tell her parents about their day trip to the beach at Great Yarmouth on the Norfolk coast. "And me put foots in sea. Tell Mama and Papa," Reggie says.

"Yes, we all waded into the sea with bare feet," Dora says, repeating Reggie's statement correctly. Now draw a nice picture for your mother and father."

Teddy concludes: I understood that we are constantly learning… Similarities and differences.

<u>Learning English</u>

Teddy observes: I watch and listen as the girls learn English at home.

Since everyone in the village speaks English, Steffi and Reggie quickly learn the new language. Immersed in an English-speaking environment they gradually switch from German to English, adapting to their new home. Dora realizes that she seldom has to explain things to the girls in German anymore, since they seem to understand most clearly spoken communication in English. Steffi learns to read and write in English. After three months, Steffi was writing to her parents in Italy in mixed German and English. *Dear eltern* (parents), *I thenk du for deinen brief* (letter). *I and Reggie have gas masks. A new tooth is coming of me. We have been to play with Patsy this morning, we wash doll clothes. Ellen gone to be Red X nurse in hospital.* Reggie drew hearts and wrote; *LOV FROM REGGIE*. Ten months after coming to England, Steffi wrote only in English: *Aunt Alice and I went to Norwich, she took me to see a man about my eyes. And Reggie and Dora met us by the bus. We hope you are well.*

When the optometrist found that Steffi was quite near-sighted she received new glasses, which made reading easier.

Every morning Aunt Alice sits with Steffi teaching her to read easy books in English and to write simple sentences. She teaches Reggie the alphabet. Dora works on counting and math facts. They all sing nursery rhymes and Aunt Alice reads to them from fairy tale books with lots of pictures. They read labels on boxes and bags as well was the signs and street names in the village.

On their walk one afternoon, Dora, Steffi and Reggie pass a building with a line of children coming out the door. Steffi looks questioningly at Dora.

"This is our village school and students are leaving for the day. The school day is over," Dora explains.

"School!" Steffi exclaims. "Why can't I go? I need to be in second grade."

"Everything is in English," Dora goes on. "You could not understand the teacher or read the textbooks."

"It's not fair! I am smart. You and Aunt Alice tell me, Papa and Mama tell me," Steffi says angrily. "I can go to school."

"I'm sorry, Steffi. You are smart, but you really could not keep up with everything in English," Dora says kindly. "The teacher does not have time to teach you separately. That's why we have lessons every day at home."

Teddy concludes: I understood that an important part of adaptation is speaking the same language.

CHAPTER 4

WAR IN ENGLAND

Sept. 3, 1939. War begins in England

Teddy observes: I sit on Steffi's lap as the family listens to the news on the big cabinet radio. I can't understand what the man is saying, but I know it is bad from watching Dora and Aunt Alice's reaction.

War again, more war! Eleven o'clock in the morning is an unusual time to turn on the radio. Both Alice and Dora lean forward in their chairs, look at each other with somber faces and anxiously listen to Prime Minister Neville Chamberlin speak. He explains that Britain is declaring war against Germany. The women bow their heads in a silent prayer.

"Is Anschluss?" Steffi asks in a low tone.

"No, no, my dear," Aunt Alice replies soothingly. "Tis not like Anschluss. Great Britain will never allow the Germans to take over our land. That is why our Prime Minister said we will go to war against the Nazis."

"Going to war means fighting to keep what you value," Dora explains further.

Steffi remembers only too well a similar occasion last year with her Papa and Mama anxiously listening to the harsh, cruel voice on the radio. She feels again the gut-wrenching fear that had gripped her while the family huddled in the cellar as the bombers flew endlessly over Vienna. Her parents' decision to send her and Reggie to safety in England followed soon afterwards. Papa and Mama had told them again and again that they would be safe in England, a free nation without war. And now here it was again! War!

Meanwhile the broadcast continues with the news that Poland, France and Australia also had declared war on Germany, while Denmark, Holland, Ireland and Spain remained neutral. No lessons today, no walks around the village, as neighbors come over to discuss the news and its implications for their lives.

When the Battle of the Atlantic begins, air raid protection procedures also start. Dora comes back from the post office and says, "We must all go to the Parish Hall on Friday at eleven. Everyone in the village will be fitted with a gas mask."

Since the girls look puzzled, she shows them pictures of gas masks in the newspaper. There are also directions for making and using black-out curtains as well as diagrams of different types of air raid shelters.

Colonel Walter and Mr. Brady have volunteered to be Air Raid Wardens for the village, Dora tells her mother. They will soon be coming around to check for lights at night.

An eerie wailing sound stops everyone. Steffi and Reggie throw themselves onto Aunt Alice sitting in her easy chair. "It's all right!" she says hugging both children to her. "They are just practicing the air raid siren in Norwich."

Dora says, "The men are coming to put up our air raid shelter in the garden at the end of the week. Then when we hear the siren, we will all go and stay in the cozy shelter until the all-clear is sounded." She does not mention the basement air raid shelters in every big building and the mass Underground subway shelters in London. Here in the country, authorities urged each family to build and stock its own air raid shelter on their property.

"Why siren? Why air raid shelter?" Steffi asks looking out the window.

"The siren is to warn people that airplanes... that German bombers might be coming," Dora states the facts with a grim face.

"Bombers?" Steffi repeats remembering Vienna.

"Yes, it is possible that bombers will fly over the village and Norwich," Dora explains, trying to comfort the children. "An air raid shelter will keep us quite safe." She doesn't tell them that bombers might target the nearby Royal Air Force Base.

Teddy concludes: I remember how it feels to be frightened by real threats and anxious about the future.

September 1939. Safe shelter

Teddy observes: I hear the air raid siren and watch the family rush to the air raid shelter.

By the time the siren's warning stops, the family including David has reached the air raid shelter in almost complete darkness. The prefabricated Anderson air raid shelter made of corrugated steel was partially buried and covered with earth and turf in the front garden.

Suddenly Steffi turns around and runs back toward the house, shouting, "Teddy, get Teddy."

Aunt Alice, just inside shelter's metal doorway, calls fearfully, "No, no! Come inside!"

"Come back at once, Steffi!" Dora orders.

"Steffi, come back!" Reggie pleads clinging to Aunt Alice.

The ominous sound of massed airplanes stops Steffi. The fearful, well-remembered sound convinces her that she must get to the shelter immediately. When the heavy door is safely closed, the adults breathe a sigh of relief. Steffi settles onto the floor beside David, while Reggie cuddles into several blankets on a cot. The lit lantern makes a cozy pool of light in the small living space. Aunt Alice and Dora had made the shelter comfortable and non-frightening with fold-up cots for sitting and sleeping, colorful cushions, and blankets. David's water bowl was crowded against a large tin box of food supplies and several bottles of water. The ever-present gas mask cases were near the door.

After weeks of frequent air raids aimed at Norwich and the nearby Royal Air Force base, the family had developed a ritual. They begin with a short prayer and then recited their favorite A.A. Milne poems together.

"Please, tonight we say Buckingham Palace," Steffi begged. They all chant in unison: "They're changing the guard at Buckingham Palace. Christopher Robin went down with Alice" from beginning to end.

"Rather ironic when the guards and the palace are being bombed nightly, wouldn't you say?" Dora whispers to her mother so the children can't hear. Her mother simply nods and opens the Winnie-the-Pooh book to where they stopped last time. "Now shall we see what adventures Pooh is having tonight?" She asks cheerily.

Teddy concludes: I understood that despite the threat there is security in the family being safely sheltered.

Christmas 1939

Teddy observes:_I watch as the family celebrates Christmas in war time.

On Christmas Eve the burning logs in the fireplace and the

fresh pine tree scent combine to smell like Christmas. Steffi and Reggie wake from a nap, as this will be a late night for them. Everyone helps to decorate the Christmas tree in the parlor. Steffi and Reggie hang ornaments, Aunt Alice drapes it with a garland of red and gold ribbons, and Dora clips on the candle holders.

"What go on top?" Steffi asks.

"This beautiful angel. It was always on top of the tree when I was a little girl," Aunt Alice says showing it to them.

Steffi says, "We have angel on tree at home also." Remembering last Christmas with Mama and Papa, she feels sad. Now her parents aren't here, only her sister. Dora senses how Steffi feels and hugs her closely.

"I think next Christmas you will be with your Mama and Papa." David comes to cuddle her too.

Later the family walks to the church for the Christmas candlelight service. The candles on the altar shine brightly in the greenery-decorated sanctuary. Everyone joins in singing *Silent Night* and *Once in royal David's city* as the organ echoes in the old stone church. The only reminder of war is the heavy blackout curtains over the stained-glass windows.

On Christmas Day Steffi and Reggie eagerly shake out their stockings and open their gifts. Christmas dinner is the traditional turkey and plum pudding is at a friend's house. But later as they sit down for tea at home, the air raid siren sounds shattering the peaceful evening. Dora grabs coats and gas masks and Aunt Alice takes the girls' hands and rushes to the air raid shelter in the garden. David guards them until the heavy door is closed.

Aunt Alice leads them in singing *Oh, Christmas tree* – the same carol, different language to *Oh, Tannenbaum* which they sang last year with Papa and Mama. But when that ends, the sound of bombers flying overhead is clear. Dora begins the chorus of "Jolly old Saint Nicholas" to drown out the sound. When the All Clear is sounded, they all go back into the house.

Earlier in December, Steffi had written an airmail letter to Mama and Papa in Italy, "I'm sorry we cannot send a card to you because it is wartime." The picture Mama had made with colored pencils in Naples arrived a few days after Christmas.

Teddy concludes: I understood the importance of maintaining Christmas traditions even in wartime, although I did not know until later that this was a world war (World War II).

Other signs of war

Teddy observes: I observe the effects of war again.

After Christmas, everyone received ration books full of coupons. There was a food shortage, since much food was imported, and German U-boats were attacking cargo ships coming to England. Now bacon, meat, butter, and sugar were rationed in the village shop. The shopkeeper cut the coupons out of the Dora's ration book when she bought two pounds of sugar or a pound of country butter. When she bought more items, she also used Aunt Alice's, Steffi and Reggie's ration books. Gas (petrol) was rationed and later even clothing was rationed.

"We are fortunate to have our own chickens?" Aunt Alice says.

"We have eggs, lots of eggs," Steffi replies.

"And we get a lot of vegetables from our garden," Dora adds as she peels home-grown potatoes.

"Carrots and peas and beans," Reggie says.

"Blackberry jam from prickly bushes."

"Apples and pears and walnuts too that we keep for winter,"

Every evening Aunt Alice pulls the heavy blackout curtains across the windows before turning on any lights. No streetlights in the village are on. Cars have a special protective hood so headlights won't show. These protocols (no visible lights) keep German bombers from locating local targets.

When Winston Churchill became Prime Minister on May tenth, 1940, he spoke on the radio. He promised 'to wage war until victory is won, and never to surrender ourselves, to servitude and shame, whatever the cost and the agony may be'.

Teddy concludes: I understood that everyone has to make adaptations when there is a war.

Preparing to reunite with parents - immigration process

Teddy observes: I watch and listen as Aunt Alice explains to Steffi and Reggie what their parents are doing.

Escaping from Nazi rule in April 1939, Steffi and Reggie left Vienna for England. Three months later their parents left Vienna for Italy. They traveled to Milan and then Genoa hoping to get work and visas to England. By September, they had learned that this was impossible. In early September, Mama wrote from Genoa, *I cannot write much to you. Hard times have come and it is bitterly hard for us that we cannot come to you.*

By November 1939, the Episcopal Committee for German Refugees in New York had found a sponsor who would provide an affidavit of support to bring the whole family to the U.S. Mama wrote from Milan, *Today we got a letter from America saying that in a short time we can all travel to America. So, we thank God and will hope that in a short time we will see you again and stay together."* But this did not happen for many months.

At the end of November, Papa wrote, *My dear good little girls, Are you happy that we will be together again? Certainly, it is difficult for you to leave good Aunt Alice and Miss Dora, David, and the chickens. But if God wishes you will see them again. It will be nice for you to come to Italy. You must be very strong on the trip.* Again on December thirtieth: *We hope to see you soon. It will not be so complicated for you to come here.*

After Christmas, in January 1940, Papa wrote from Milan, *Today we obtained the papers for America. You know it is easier if we sail together, so you must accept the little difficulties of travel to Italy, I hope one of the Friends will see that you are accompanied by a good lady. We will await you at the Italian frontier.*

But Steffi and Reggie did not travel to Italy to meet their Papa and Mama.

January 22, 1940.

Telegram from the Germany Emergency Committee in London to the parents in Milan.

STRONGLY RECOMMEND CHILDREN REMAIN HERE. REUNITE IN AMERICA. TRANSIT VISA FRANCE ALMOST IMPOSSIBLE.

February 16, 1940.

Airmail letter from the American Committee for Christian Refugees in New York to the parents in Milan. *Our correspondent in London has informed us quite finally that the war conditions preclude (stop) the sending of the children to Italy, so you will have to proceed to the U.S. in advance of the children.*

April 20-29, 1940,

Papa and Mama travel from Naples to New York on a ship, the S.S. Washington. Their nine-day trip across the Atlantic left the war in Europe behind. They immediately informed the Movement for the Care of Children from Germany of their arrival and filed Form 575 for their children to immigrate to the U.S.

Teddy concludes: I understood that the parents were doing everything possible to reunite safely with their children in the U.S.

August 1940. London

Teddy observes: I listen to Steffi talking about their visit to London.

Aunt Alice and Dora took Steffi and Reggie to London for an interview at the American Consulate. Dressed in their best dresses, they took the train from Norwich to London. After completing the official business at the American Consul's office in Bloomsbury, they rode a red double-decker bus to St. James Park near Buckingham Palace. Steffi and Reggie had begged to see the changing of the guard at Buckingham Palace. Since the royal residence was now surrounded by sandbags, it was almost impossible to glimpse the red-uniformed guards at their sentry posts. They could see the blackened windows where the palace had been bombed. Reminded of the danger of bombing in London, Aunt Alice and Dora decided to return home without any more sightseeing.

At home, Steffi told Teddy about their visit to London. She said, "All the people at the office were very nice, but I held on to Dora's hand. Reggie held on to Aunt Alice." She hunched her shoulders as she said, "It was scary to see where Buckingham Palace was bombed."

Teddy concludes: I understood that the trip to London was a necessary part of the process of reuniting the children with their parents.

September 30, 1940. The slow post

Teddy observes: I watch an emotional scene.

Aunt Alice, usually so calm and serene, was visibly upset about something, "We've had a letter... But it's too late. The children cannot..."

"What's happened?" Dora asks anxiously.

"They've missed the boat!" Aunt Alice exclaims, "Today's the thirtieth."

Dora's voice shakes as she reads the official letter, "The guardians of Stephanie and Regina Dush are requested to bring them to the London Office of The Friends Service Committee on September twenty-fifth ready for departure for the United States of America. Officials there will then take responsibility for their safe departure via ship."

"Just think, if the Committee had sent a telegram instead of a letter, you would be on a ship crossing the ocean at this very moment," Aunt Alice says. "I'm so glad you missed the boat!"

"Missed the boat!" Steffi repeats, bursting into tears. The full realization that she and Reggie were to leave this home, this safe, friendly, comfortable nest with Aunt Alice and Dora and David had finally dawned on her.

"Leave home!" Reggie says piteously with her lip trembling. Tears roll down the cheeks of the two adults, as the children sob and cling to them. The idea of leaving home once again seems too hard to bear.

"We must notify the Office immediately and tell them what

has happened," Dora states. "We must explain that their letter dated the twentieth of September only arrived here today, the thirtieth."

With a gasp, Dora remembers something and finds yesterday's newspaper. There it is – the lead article.

CHILDREN BRAVE IN BOATS DESPITE CRIES AND MOANS OF DYING, ESCORTS REPORT. The few survivors of the British refugee ship on which 293 persons lost their lives told tales of heroism. In the North Atlantic the convoy HX-72 was successfully attacked by a U-boat group over the course of a three-day period. Altogether 12 ships of 78,000 tons were sunk, seven of them during the night of Sept. 27-28 by Schepeke's U-100 without being detected by the convoy escorts.

Aunt Alice collapses on a chair, her face white with shock. "They would have been on that ship! Our little Reggie and Steffi!"

"Mother, you were right to be happy that they missed the boat," Dora exclaims. Then with the same idea in mind, both mother and daughter kneel down to pray, thanking God for sparing the lives of the two well-loved children.

Teddy concludes: I understood that Steffi and Reggie were alive only by the grace of God.

October 24, 1940. Preparing to leave home

Teddy observes: I watch Dora and Aunt Alice pack and listen to the conversation.

The suitcases are packed, the new backpacks are ready. Steffi still can't quite believe it. "We're going on a trip without you and Dora, just me and Reggie."

"Yes, but at the end of the trip you will be with your dear

mother and father," Aunt Alice says comfortingly.

A couple of days later, Aunt Alice receives a telegram from the London Committee. The children are to leave on the next convoy, time and place strictly censored. Their friend Mrs. Elling will drive Steffi and Reggie straight to a boarding school south of London where they will wait and be taken to the ship. Steffi and Reggie have new cloth backpacks made by Aunt Alice. Teddy is safely tucked inside Steffi's bag, and Reggie has Jemima Puddle Duck in hers. Steffi and Reggie as well as Aunt Alice and Dora are crying as they say good-bye. Everyone is sad at parting.

Steffi thinks; Good-bye again. On our own again. Traveling again. Anxiety sets in.

Teddy concludes: I understood that we were leaving home again and the children would be traveling across the ocean on a ship to reunite with their parents.

Note: Telegrams were sent by cable to a Western Union telegraph office. The message was transmitted by Morse code, then typed on a typewriter, put in an envelope with the recipient's address and delivered by a messenger on a bike. Western Union provided 'cable service to all the world'.

CHAPTER 5

TRANSITIONS ACROSS THE ATLANTIC OCEAN

<u>October 30, 1940. Waiting to leave – between homes and countries</u>

Teddy observes: this is my first opportunity to watch other children and teachers at a school.

Aunt Alice's friend, Mrs. Elling drives Steffi and Reggie to Parson's Mead School in Surrey and escorts them in with their luggage. When Mrs. Elling leaves, Steffi and Reggie are with strangers in a new place once again.

The Headmistress greets the girls. "Welcome to our school. You will stay here and take classes with the other children who are waiting for the ship to depart."

It's all new, but Steffi relishes her first taste of school life and the anxious feeling slowly disappears. With a dozen or so other refugee children waiting for the next ship, she and Reggie have lessons in the science room with one of the junior mistresses. Sitting at a school desk, Steffi understands the teacher's directions, and finds the math exercises easy. She happily completes reading assignments of familiar stories. She becomes friends with two girls, Frieda and Angela. When letters arrive from Dora and Aunt Alice, she writes back to tell them about her new experiences.

After a week at the school, an official takes all the refugee children to the ship in a limousine.

Teddy concludes: I understood that the children were going on another longer journey leaving England for America.

Nov. 14, 1940. Aboard ship

Teddy observes: I watch and listen to Steffi, Reggie, the new lady, and girl in the ship's cabin.

Four people were in the small cabin with its two sets of bunk beds – Steffi and Reggie and Mrs. Whitby and Pamela. Mrs. Whitby, who was returning to New York with her daughter Pamela, was in charge of eight-year old Steffi and six-year-old Reggie. A responsible adult passenger had agreed to look after each of the refugee children from Parsons Mead. They were among the three hundred and fifty passengers traveling tourist class on the Cunard White Star liner, Samaria.

"May I go to lounge?" Steffi asked Mrs. Whitby. "I think I can see friends from school there." Steffi was referring to other refugee children she'd met at Parsons Mead. Steffi ran to the end of the corridor and opened the double doors into the large, shabby lounge. People were sitting at tables playing cards, others were reading or chatting, but Steffi quickly spotted two girls who had been at Parsons Mead. They were looking at a map laid flat on a desk.

"We are trying to trace how the ship is traveling," Frieda explained when Steffi joined them.

"Well, here is Liverpool," Angela pointed at the city on Mersey Bay.

"Yes, we got on – we boarded ship – at Liverpool," Steffi

said. "But where is Parsons Mead at Ashstead? I thought it was near London."

"Here," Frieda pointed out. "Here it is in Surrey, just southwest of London. We had to travel North-Northwest from there to get to Liverpool."

"That's why it took so long in that big car," Steffi said beginning to understand the distance across England. "Let me see if I can find Norwich."

"Do you remember when we stopped at Cobh and some people got on?" Frieda asked the others. "Here it is on the English Channel."

"That's in Ireland," Steffi pointed out.

A blue uniformed steward saw the children studying the map. He asked if they wanted help in tracing the ship's route. He kindly showed them the Samaria's northerly route across the Atlantic. He also explained that they would stop in Boston before arriving at their final destination in New York.

Steffi was fascinated. "Please, can we find Austria too. That's where I came from."

"Ah, here it is." The children's eyes and fingers moved to the right on the large world map. Soon each of the young refugees was finding his hometown and tracing her own trip to England.

Days later as they packed for the arrival in New York, Steffi whispered to Reggie, "We will see Papa and Mama tomorrow. It is a long time ago that we saw them." She was feeling anxious because she could hardly remember Papa's face or Mama's smile. The loving, determinedly cheerful words from their letters echoed in her head, but not their voices. It had been a year and a half since the good-bye at the train station in Vienna. Her role as big sister kept her from talking to Reggie about her fears. So, Steffi tried to replace the images of Miss Kraus on the train from

43

Vienna, Aunt Alice and Dora, Mrs. Elling and the nice teacher at Parsons Mead, with those of her own mother and father.

"What if they don't know me? I wear my glasses now," she worried.

"You write about your glasses, and Dora too," her little sister reassured her. "They will know you and me." Reggie had no doubt about that.

But what happened next, completely overshadowed that worry.

Teddy concludes: I understood that the purpose of this long journey was to reunite a family

CHAPTER 6

BETWEEN HOMES IN AMERICA

November 20, 1940. Arrival in the U.S.

Teddy observes: I watch and listen trying to understand why Papa and Mama aren't there to meet us.

But it was not Mama or Papa who meet us when we arrive in New York Harbor. The large port arrivals building is full of people greeting each other, holding up signs and pushing luggage carts. A tall man greets us at a check-in desk, "Hello, hello! You must be Steffi and Reggie. Your mother and father asked me to meet you. I am Dr. Carper and you will stay with my family for a little while." His kind smile helps a little to dispel Steffi's shock – Mama and Papa are not there.

"We left our cozy home with Dora and Aunt Alice to be with Mama and Papa and they aren't here. It isn't fair! Why?" So many questions rush through Steffi's mind, so much bewilderment as she holds tightly to Reggie's hand.

As Dr. Carper drives them through the strange new world of Brooklyn Brownstones, he tells them more. "Your mother and father stayed with me and my family when they arrived from Italy. Your parents are fine people and they want to see you as soon as possible."

As soon as possible, but not here and now. "Where are my Mama and Papa?" Steffi asks Dr. Carper. "Are they at your house?"

"No, they are now in Glendale, Ohio staying at a farm. They are adjusting to life in the United States." He went on to explain that Ohio is a state that is further west of the state of New York where the sisters are now.

It was only much later that Steffi and Reggie fully understood the situation. Due to the trauma of leaving home and country, seeking asylum for this family, difficulty of selling his patents for financial security, attempting to maintain dignity and self-worth, Papa became paranoid. He went into a sanatorium for a short period to regain mental stability. Today his condition might rather be diagnosed as PTSD (Post traumatic stress disorder). Mama had to remain separated from her husband to maintain her own mental health.

Teddy concludes: I understood that a parental substitute met the children when they arrived on the ship from England.

November 1940. A new home in Brooklyn

Teddy observes: I watch Steffi and Reggie adapt to life in Brooklyn

Dr. and Mrs. Carper were kind and caring, but their daughters, Mary and Betty really made everything easier. Twelve-year-old Mary and ten-year-old Betty helped Steffi and Reggie learn about the house, the neighborhood and best of all school. Steffi was finally going to a real school – she was in third grade in P.S 198.

"It's a good thing we learned to speak English," Steffi explained to Mary and Betty. "We only knew German before - in Austria."

"I guess they speak English in England," Betty said teasing.

"Yes, and read and write in English," Steffi teased back. "English, English, English!"

The brownstone houses and tall buildings and downstairs shops in Brooklyn were very different from the two cities Steffi and Reggie knew... Very different from Norwich, quite different from Vienna. But going to the store with Mrs. Carper was similar to going shopping with Dora. And the bustle of traffic on the streets reminded her of downtown Vienna. Now for the first time Steffi encountered people from many different countries, different races and languages. She observed mothers pushing prams, boys playing ball, kids riding bikes, ladies with shopping bags chatting on the sidewalk. Streets were lined with small shops, corner grocery stores and street vendors selling food from push carts. So busy - so much going on always.

School was everything Steffi had ever dreamed of and much more. Every day she proudly walked to P.S one hundred and ninety-eight beside Betty and lined up outside the curb-side building to go down the long hall to her classroom. She sat at her desk in a neat row of third grade students and learned to fill in the answers on purple mimeographed worksheet. She memorized lists of spelling words and took Friday spelling tests. She listened to the teacher as she wrote on the blackboard at the front of the room and raised her hand when she knew the answer to a question. She ran around with the other kids at recess in the school courtyard. She was happy not to be the only girl who wore glasses and was glad she wasn't the only student who came from another country. Keeping up with assignments was easy. In addition, Mary and Betty played school with her and first-grade Reggie every afternoon as they did their homework.

Mama and Papa's absence somehow faded into all the new experiences.

Church services in Vienna, England and in New York were similar, but different. Attending St. Stephens Cathedral in Vienna (before the Nazi take-over) had been awe-inspiring for six-year-old Steffi. The Anglican Church in their English village had felt warm and familiar with its hymns and pews filled with neighbors. Now here in Brooklyn the four girls attended Sunday School at the Flatbush Presbyterian Church, while their elders attended the church service. Instead of sitting in pews in the church listening to the priest, the children sit around tables in the sunny Sunday School classroom listening to the teacher. In December, Steffi received a certificate for 'perfect memory work'.

December's snow in Brooklyn also produced familiar sensations and images. The general feeling of a snowy day, the touch of snowflakes on your face, the crunch of snowflakes under foot, the molding of snow into balls – the same in each country or continent. N

Steffi watched Dr. and Mrs. Carper read the news of the war in Europe in the New York Times and listen to the news on the radio.

"Papa and Mama read the newspaper in German. Aunt Alice and Dora read English newspapers," Steffi recalled. "And here Dr. and Mrs. Carper read the American paper."

"Everybody listened to the radio too," Reggie said.

"How else would we know what those bad Nazis are doing?" Steffi mused.

There are lots of church connections. The Quakers sponsored the Kindertransport. Aunt Alice was the widow and Dora the daughter of an Anglican priest. Dr. Carper, a pastor was the head of an organization which united all Brooklyn's Protestant churches. Miss Jackson, their sponsor to the U.S. was strongly allied to the Episcopal Church.

48

Teddy concludes: I understood that children are resilient, adapting to changing situations.

Christmas 1940 in Brooklyn

Teddy observes: We celebrate Christmas in a third country in three years with some of the same but also new traditions.

Three Christmases in three different countries: 1938 in Vienna; 1939 in an English village, and 1940 in Brooklyn, New York. But, Santa Claus was very similar to Sankt Nicolaus and Saint Nicholas, and there were always gifts, Christmas dinner and a special Christmas church service.

On Christmas morning, Steffi and Reggie along with Mary and Betty looked in their Christmas stockings, excited to see what Santa had left them. There were more presents than they'd ever had before – from the Carpers and church ladies, from Dora and Aunt Alice and from Mama. Also, a first – a long-distance telephone call from Papa. Steffi recognized his voice immediately, though he sounded different speaking in English over the phone.

Teddy concludes: Christmas traditions are similar in different countries and families.

March 1941. Time to leave

Teddy observes: I watch the packing of suitcases once again.

As winter turned to spring, the comfortable routines were disrupted by yet another departure. Now almost-nine-year old Steffi helped with packing the battered suitcases. After six secure months with the Carpers, she was more accepting of yet another change, another journey. She and Reggie were going to Cincinnati, Ohio to join Mama. Most comforting was that this time Dr. Carper would accompany them on the train trip instead of a stranger. But it was hard saying goodbye to their new friends Betty and Mary and to kind Mrs. Carper and their life in Brooklyn.

The train from New York's Grand Central Station took them west through New Jersey, across the width of Pennsylvania to Columbus, Ohio and then south to Cincinnati. Dr. Carper told the girls about the places they passed and explained the changing terrain. This was Steffi and Reggie's first view of their new country beyond urban Brooklyn.

Teddy concludes: I understood that the children were again traveling to a secure location to reunite with their parents.

<u>April 1941 the children's home, Cincinnati, Ohio</u>

Teddy observes: I see how disappointed the children are at not joining their parents immediately.

Dr. Carper left Steffi and Reggie, not with their mother, but in the efficient hands of Matron of the Children's Home. She led them to a dormitory where there were a dozen beds.

"This is where you will sleep," Matron said. "This room is for girls who are here temporarily. The rest of this building houses orphans."

Steffi sat on the bed beside Reggie feeling totally dejected. Only minutes but it seemed like hours later, a girl came and told them their mother was there to see them.

"I was hoping to be there when my daughters arrived,"

Mama said breathlessly." But I had to take two streetcars to get here. It took longer than I thought." Mama was apologizing to Matron for being late.

And there was Mama, (looking different, but still Mama) hugging and kissing Steffi and Reggie over and over again. It was a moment of pure joy – mother and children finally together again. Tears and joyful smiles at being reunited at long last.

Steffi was happy but full of questions, "Why didn't you meet us when we got here? Where's Papa? Why are we sleeping here?"

"First let me look at you," Mama said smiling. "You've grown so much, my Steffi. And my little Reggie, you are a big girl now too."

Reggie was talking non-stop, seemingly wanting to make up for all the time they'd been apart. Finally, Mama was able to explain the situation. She told her girls about their Papa's mental illness, a result of immigration, but didn't give any details. So, Steffi was still left wondering about her big strong Papa. Mama told them that she was living in one room in a boarding house, so they had to stay at the Children's Home until she found a job and an apartment.

It was only when Matron announced that visiting hours were over, that their conversation ended. Mama promised to come again soon.

On Steffi's ninth birthday, she received cards from all the Carpers, Aunt Alice and Dora as well as from Mama. Mama's card had a picture of a birthday cake with the words - I baked this birthday cake for you. (Mama wrote in cursive *but only in thought*. How sad that they couldn't be together on this birthday in their new country!

Teddy concludes: I understood that the children had to live in the

Children's Home until their mother could provide a home for them.

March 8 to June 12, 1941. School.

Teddy observes: I hear Steffi talk about school.

Steffi and Reggie marched to Oakley School with the other children from the Home. Steffi was continuing in third grade and Reggie in first. Steffi wrote spelling test words on small strips of notebook paper with a pencil, while she wrote dictation on notebook paper cut in half.

They adapted to the new routines, eating their meals in the dining room, going to bed when 'bedtime' was called, goi ng to school on weekdays, seeing Mama on weekends. They lived by these strict routines with no variations until measles struck. Several girls in their dorm had disappeared and some students in their classes were missing.

One morning, Steffi woke up, feeling feverish, with a runny nose and a sore throat. As soon as Matron saw her at breakfast, she took Steffi to the Infirmary.

Teddy concludes: I understood that children thrive on routines

The infirmary in the children's home

Teddy observes: I listen and watch all that is going on.

The large brightly lit room was full of children in small hospital beds lined up in two neat rows. Reddish rash-covered arms and faces stood out in sharp contrast to the white sheets and hospital gowns worn by each child. The smell of antiseptic hung in the air of the big room which seemed hygienic and cold.

"Open your mouth!" The white-capped nurse by Steffi's bed held out a thermometer.

"After you take my temperature, can I go talk to my sister?" Steffi asked pointing to a bed across the room. "I can see she's crying."

"Don't you know the rules?" The nurse asked sternly. "You get out of bed to go to the bathroom, nothing else. Now open your mouth!"

The nurses were crisp and efficient, but not warm and caring and rules were strictly enforced. The sign outside the infirmary door read: *Warning: measles*. This section of the infirmary was in quarantine because of a measles epidemic at the Children's Home. Steffi and Reggie and the other girls and boys who were infected by the highly contagious virus were quarantined here for at least fourteen days.

Some patients napped, several hid under their covers, some wept, a few like Steffi read books, but there was almost no childish chatter. Nurses made their rounds, maids brought meals on trays, janitors mopped the floor, aides bathed the children. At first this all seemed strange, but itsoon became the daily routine.

When screens were hastily put around a bed, a doctor rushed in – everyone in the room was scared and cried. Nurse announced loudly, "Not to worry. Our friend here is just having a bit of a bad spell."

Fourteen days of this – no real comfort or loving care, just hope that the rash and fever would disappear quickly and the measles would be gone.

I want to get out of here, I want to get out of here; the refrain kept going through Steffi's head. "We need to get to Mama." Steffi was not only itchy and uncomfortable on the thin mattress, but felt lost and lonely and worried about Reggie. Her sole escape was in the stories she read avidly (library books were generously provided).

Teddy concludes: Fortunately, the children's stay in the infirmary was brief.

Note: It was not until 1963 that the measles vaccine appeared and children no longer had to suffer through this disease.

CHAPTER 7

AT HOME WITH MAMA IN OHIO

June 1941. Apartment in Cincinnati.

Teddy observes: I am happy to see Steffi and Reggie living with Mama again.

At last, after three months in the Children's Home, Steffi and Reggie and Mama were living together in a small apartment in downtown Cincinnati. They all spoke English now; German was left behind in Austria. Mama worked for a dress company as a seamstress and Steffi and Reggie attended the nearby Fairview School. After the routines at the Children's Home, daily life in the one-bedroom apartment was more unpredictable. Everyone had to adjust to work and summer school schedules, trips to the corner grocery store and the library.

Steffi and Reggie were overwhelmed by the emotional meeting with Papa for the first time after two years. Mama discretely left them alone and didn't talk about it later. Papa had just moved to Cincinnati after working in Chicago for half a year. After that, Papa's visits were always unannounced and somewhat chaotic. Sometimes he took them to a park or best of all to the zoo. He told them about his work and the new machine he had invented and was patenting. Reggie longed to live with Papa, while Steffi was content with Mama.

One hot summer night, Steffi and Reggie both shrieked in

terror as something black flew around near the ceiling of their room. Reggie screamed, "What's that?"

"It's a bat. They fly in the window sometimes." Mama explained and pointed to the wide-open, unscreened window. They all watched the bat as it finally stopped circling and settled on top of a cabinet. It took some time for Mama finally to usher the bat out. Steffi quickly shut and locked the window to make sure it wouldn't return. "It's really hot in here and we need fresh air. Let's leave the window open just a little," Mama said. "Now we have a bat story we can tell."

Steffi remembered this bat incident, when Mama told them that they were moving to Bat Cave, North Carolina.

Teddy observes: I understood that everyone adapted to a new life style.

Grandmother left in Europe.

Teddy observes: I watch as Mama looks through the envelopes that arrive in the mail.

Steffi knew that Mama was worried. Every day, Mama watched the mail hopefully, and was sad when there was no letter from her mother.

"Is Grandmama all right?" Steffi asked.

"I don't know, I just don't know." Mama replied anxiously.

"We got letters from her in England," Steffi recalls.

"I haven't heard from her since we were in Italy," Mama says. "I keep hoping the mail is just slow in coming to a new address."

Reggie tries to comfort her mother with a hug. "Maybe it's hard for her to write. Maybe the Nazis don't let the mail go out."

"I tried to contact her friend but no answer," Mama says. "Now I think I will ask Miss Jackson for help in contacting my mother, your Grandmama."

"That's a good idea."

Teddy concludes: I understood a person's anxiety in not having had any communication with her mother.

Dec. 8, 1941. War begins in America.

Teddy observes: I watch and listen to the radio again.

War again. When Mama turned on the radio in the apartment, they all sat around it listening. President Roosevelt (FDR) was speaking to Congress and the American people.

"Yesterday, December seventh 1941 — a date which will live in infamy — the United States of America was suddenly and deliberately attacked by naval and air forces of the Empire of Japan.

"I ask that the Congress declare that since the unprovoked and dastardly attack by Japan on Sunday, December seventh, 1941, a state of war has existed between the United States and the Japanese Empire."

On December 7, 1941, Japanese bombers attacked Pearl Harbor, a U.S.A military base in Hawaii. More than two thousand four hundred Americans were killed. Before Pearl Harbor, a war with Japan had seemed likely but the attack made the U.S. declare war.

Now the war they had left behind in Europe had begun here in their new safe land. The Axis powers – Germany, Italy and Japan were now at war with most of the world... World War II. By May sixth, 1942 the family had received a War Ration Book

1 with war ration stamps. Mama and now Steffi read the newspaper daily for news of the war.

Mama opened the mail one day in May and there was a war ration book one for each of them.

"We had ration books that Dora took to the store?" Steffi told Mama. "They took out the stamps when you bought things like sugar."

"Yes, of course, England had rationing when the war started there," Mama said. "Now we have rationing here too."

All Americans were asked to help with the war effort by buying defense savings bonds and stamps in addition to rationing. Everyone received war ration books for food items including sugar, meat, dairy, coffee, dried fruits, jams, jellies, lard, shortening, and oils. In addition, automobiles, tires, gasoline, fuel oil, coal, firewood, nylon, silk, and shoes were rationed. Since supplies of raw materials such as rubber and tin were cut off by the enemy, there were national scrap drives to collect rubber, tin cans, paper and metal. V for victory was the slogan, and people were encouraged to plant a victory garden. Blackout regulations were for east and west coast states but didn't affect other parts of the country like here in Ohio. The family used war ration book one and two while living in the apartment on Vine Street in Cincinnati. They received war ration book three in Bat Cave, North Carolina.

The war ended on the western front when Germany surrendered on May ninth, 1945, Victory in Europe Day (V-E Day) and on the eastern front when Japan surrendered on August 14, 1945.

Teddy concludes: I understood once again the constraints that war imposes on everyone.

<u>1942-43. School.</u>

Teddy observes: I watch what Steffi studies in school.

Steffi was learning about Colonial history in fourth grade at Fairview School. She was excited to hear that the early settlers came from England. "Just like we did, only it took us one week while it took months for the sailing ships to cross the Atlantic."

Steffi loved everything about school except that teachers, and other students, called her by her full name Stephanie rather than Steffi.

Steffi took the top off her fountain pen and began a page of handwriting practice in her notebook. "Oh, no!" Steffi said to herself as a blob of ink smeared the line of q's she was writing.

"Is this your neatest work, Stephanie?" The teacher asked disapprovingly.

She tried to write neatly as she quickly completed the purple mimeographed worksheet before the bell rang. Since Russia was a U.S. ally, all the fifth grade students including Steffi had a Russian pen pal.

Teddy concludes: I understood that students learn many different things in school.

<u>Summer 1943. Moving south.</u>

Teddy observes: I understand that more changes are coming.

After Mama and Papa were divorced in April 1943, Mama decided to move out of Cincinnati. She and her daughters would go from mid-eastern Ohio to east coast North Carolina. They would move from a big city to a small mountain village. Steffi and Reggie studied a U.S. map to find a route from Ohio south through Kentucky and Tennessee, to the Blue Ridge Mountains in western North Carolina.

Teddy concludes: I understood that Mama and the girls were moving away from the city to a small village.

CHAPTER 8

AT HOME IN NORTH CAROLINA

1943. At home in Bat Cave, North Carolina.

Teddy observes: I learn about a very different environment.

The wood-shingled house was on the side of a mountain... Steffi, Reggie and Mama's new home was in Bat Cave in the mountains of North Carolina. Eleven-year-old Steffi and nine-year old Reggie were going from a city to a village once again. But this small house on a mountain was completely different from the English village where they lived with Aunt Alice and Dora.

Bat Cave village was in Hickory Nut Gorge where three highways merged, US Route 64, US Rout 74A, and NC 9 which went from Black Mountain, past Bat Cave to Chimney Rock and Lake Lure, where the school was located.

"Where are the bats?" Reggie asked standing on the back porch the first night. "This place is called Bat Cave. Right?"

"I read that there is a cave with lots of bats in Blue Rock Mountain near here," Steffi said. "That's why the first settlers called it Bat Cave."

"I'd be scared to go in there," Reggie said remembering the bat incident.

"No one can go in," Steffi said. "The article said the bats in that cave are endangered, so it's a protected area."

The family walked everywhere in Bat Cave. At first, it was

down the mountain to go to the store and post office. Later when they moved down to a house near the river, mother and daughters walked to church and to visit neighbors. The family went for long walks along the river watching for fish jumping and birds flying. They learned about new plants like the invasive kudzu vines.

"We used to walk like this with Dora," Steffi remembered. "We walked along the Broads looking for cattails and nesting birds."

"And this river is Broads too, the Broad River," Reggie said.

"That's interesting, two rivers named Broad," Mama replied. "Do you remember walking along the Danube River with me and Papa when you were little?"

"It was very, very wide with boats," Steffi recalled.

"I had my hair cut very short and my head was cold," Reggie said touching her shoulder length brown hair. "I remember that!"

Mama, Steffi and Reggie waited at the bus stop in front of the Bat Cave post office for a bus to the town of Hendersonville fifteen miles south. Steffi said, "You know, Mama, this is almost like in England. We always had to wait for the bus to the closest city – that's Norwich."

"Well, if we want to go to the library and get new shoes, we have to go to town," Mama said. "That's necessary when you live in a small village with just one general store."

"So, we take the bus to Hendersonville," Reggie added.

Teddy concludes: I understood that the family was again adapting to a different place and life style.

Riding to school on a school bus.

Teddy observes: I watch the children riding a school bus to a distant school for the first time.

Although Bat Cave is in Henderson County, the nearest elementary school was at Lake Lure in Rutherford County six miles away. Riding a school bus was a totally new experience for Steffi and Reggie. Their first school experience had been the several block walk to P.S. 198 in Brooklyn with Betty and Mary. Then they walked to Fairview in Cincinnati. Now the fifth and sixth graders waited for the school bus at a stop near their house and rode the school bus with other students on the long, winding road to Lake Lure School.

"Why can't we have paper lunch bags like the other girls?" Steffi asked her mother.

"You have a very nice lunch box that snaps shut," Mama said.

"And why can't I have delicious smelling fried things? They make their bags shiny and smell so good," Steffi complained.

"I give you healthy food for lunch, so be glad for that," Mama answered.

Steffi felt that she was the only sixth grader in Lake Lure School who didn't speak with a Southern accent. She knew for sure that she was the only new student, and definitely the only one who came from another state, much less another country.

One recess Steffi was with a group of giggling girls. They were whispering – telling dirty jokes and at the punch-line everyone laughed. Although Steffi had no idea what they were saying, she laughed loudly. She thought, I don't want them to think I don't understand it. I don't want to be different. Steffi wanted desperately to fit in.

Steffi and Reggie attended Lake Lure School for two years, from seventh through seventh grade which is Now Lake Lure Classical Academy, a charter school. For eighth and ninth grade, Steffi and Reggie went to Edneyville School a mere four-mile school bus ride from Bat Cave. By ninth grade, Steffi really felt part of her class and was elected Class Secretary

Steffi wasn't aware at the time that there were only white kids at their schools and that all the teachers were White. The only Blacks were the janitor and the kitchen lady. She certainly didn't know that schools were segregated and that they attended a white-only school. In North Carolina, there were separate schools for Black children and for American Indian children, taught by teachers of the same race, trained in separate colleges.

Teddy concludes: I understood that children don't want to be different from others.

Bookworm

Teddy observes: I see that Steffi loves to read wherever she is.

"You're a bookworm," Reggie teases her sister.

"I am not a worm!" Steffi responds indignantly. "I just like to read... I don't eat the pages, I read them."

Steffi was sitting against a tree in the yard engrossed in Little Women. The bookshelf in the living room was filling up with books, as birthday and Christmas gifts always included books. Library books from school and the Hendersonville Public Library were a constant source of new literature. Through fiction, Steffi met new characters and creatures from all over the world as her imagination soared.

Teddy concludes: I understood how important reading is.

CHAPTER 9

THE SECOND WORLD WAR ENDS

March 26, 1945. War ends.

Teddy observes: I listen with the family to the news on the small radio.

Mama, seventh-grade Steffi and sixth-grade Reggie sit close to the radio listening to the news. The month-long Battle of Iwo Jima was over. U.S. Marines and Navy had landed on and eventually captured the island of Iwo Jima from the Imperial Japanese Army. Sadly, many Americans died to gain this victory.

May 9, 1945. Mama, Steffi and Reggie are, once again, huddled around the radio. This time there was good news - news of surrender, news that one part of the war was finally over. Germany had surrendered to the Allies. It was V-E Day, Victory in Europe Day.

July 2, 1945. The family listen to the news in their Bat Cave home. The U.S. won the ninety-eight -day Battle of Okinawa. This major battle of the Pacific War was fought on the island of Okinawa by Army and Marines against the Imperial Japanese Army.

Note: No one could predict that then thirteen-year old, 7th grade Steffi of Bat Cave would later meet and marry then eighteen-year *old Pal of Brooklyn, Marine bow gunner in the 1st Tank Battalion of Okinawa.*

July 26, 1945. The Allies (the Big Three Allies: Great Britain, Soviet Union, and U.S.) call for the unconditional surrender of the Imperial Japanese armed forces in the Potsdam Declaration. The alternative is 'prompt and utter destruction'. Japan ignored the ultimatum.

Aug. 6-9, 1945. Everybody was talking about the first use of nuclear weapons by the Allies. The U.S. Army had dropped atomic bombs on the Japanese Islands of Hiroshima and Nagasaki.

Aug. 15, 1945. The Japanese officially surrender to the Allies. World War II had finally ended.

"It's finally over – seven years of war!" Mama said, "Do you remember the bombers flying overhead at the Anschluss in Vienna in 1938 and how scared we were?"

"Yes, Mama, and Kristallnacht at Grandmama's," Steffi added. "And then we went to England."

"And then the bombing started there, and we had to go into the air raid shelter when the bombers came," Reggie recalled.

"And then we came here, and before long Japan bombed Pearl Harbor," Steffi recalled.

"Yes, we've experienced seven years of war in different countries, but thank God it's over now," Mama concluded.

One lasting effect of these experiences was that Reggie routinely hid under a pillow when she heard a plane flying overhead.

"And now let us pray for all the people who were killed, all the military, all the civilians, all the victims of the war."

"Just like we do in church on Sunday," Steffi said.

Mama, Steff and Reggie bowed their heads and folded their hands in prayer.

Teddy concludes: I understood that this long world war was finally over.

1946. A lost grandmother.

Teddy observes: I watch the family reading a fateful letter.

When Mama opened the envelope and read the contents, she began crying heartbrokenly.

"What happened, Mama?"

"What's wrong?" She couldn't speak but held out the letter from Grandmama's friend so Steffi could read it.

"Oh, my God, she died in a concentration camp."

It was only later that they learned all the details. Grandmama (who was seventy-one) was taken from her home in Vienna to the camp at Terezín, Czechoslovakia in 1942. She lived in that camp for two years and then was sent to the Auschwitz Concentration Camp in Poland. How long she survived that death camp is unknown. But that's where our dear grandmother died.

Prisoner of Ghetto Theresienstadt (1941-1945) Database.

Reg. number:	Death: yes
Family Name: Flesch	Date:
First Name: Anna	Coffin no.:
Sex: F	Coroner cert.:
Birth date:01.02.1871	Survived: no
Last address:	Other camps:
Country: Austria	1.

City: Wein 1	2.
Street: Fleischmarkt 20/7	3.
Transport to Terezin	Transport from Terezin
Number: IV/7 198	Number: DZ 1595
Date: 14.08.1942	Date: 15.05.1944
From Country: Austria	Destination: Aushwitz
City: Wein (Vienna)	

It was worse than we had feared.

"The last letter I ever got from my mother was when we were in Italy. I had begged her to leave Vienna with us. I was afraid of what could happen to her… And the worst did happen," Mama cried bitterly.

Steffi and Reggie hugged their mother, trying to comfort her.

"On the day before we left for Italy, I remember saying to her, I will see you again soon."

"But you never did," Reggie said softly.

"I tried so many times, so many different ways to contact her after she stopped writing," Mama said, crying.

Steffi went to get something to show her mother. "Grandmama sent these handkerchiefs to us in England. Aunt Alice thought they were beautifully made."

Then Mama went to rummage through the things that she'd brought from Vienna and Italy. "Here's the picture of my mother when she was a young bride," Mama said. "And here's her last letter."

Steffi and Reggie looked at the thin airmail page, remembering their letters from Grandmama. Mama said sadly, "I will always hold in my heart one sentence she wrote; "I want to give you my blessing in a quiet prayer."

"I will never forget being with Grandmama at Kristallnacht,

and how she helped me not to be scared," Steffi recalled.

Drying her tears, Reggie said, "I remember when Grandmama came to our house and we showed her our toys."

"And I remember my fifth birthday when she gave me Teddy," Steffi said setting him in her lap, "And here he is."

"So, Teddy is always a reminder of your dear Grandmama.

"A living memory... Just look at his kind eyes, just like hers."

Teddy concludes: We grieve for loved ones who died and cherish our memories of them.

Theresienstadt was a Nazi Germany's concentration camp and ghetto from November 24, 1941 to May 9, 1945. Jews were sent to the concentration camp and kept there until they were sent to an extermination camp, where they were killed. The ghetto was called a 'retirement settlement' for older Jews. This description was used as propaganda to make people think this was a nice place. The Nazi's real goal was the Final Solution (killing all Jews).

Auschwitz was Nazi Germany's largest concentration camp and extermination camp. Auschwitz was actually three camps in one: a prison camp, an extermination camp, and a slave-labor camp. Between 1.1 and 1.5 million people died there; ninety percent of them were Jews.

An illegal border-crossing story.

Teddy observes: I listen in amazement as Mama tells us a story from Italy.

Mama had been reluctant to talk about her and Papa's time

in Italy. All that teen-age Steffi and Reggie knew about it was from Mama and Papa's cheerful letters and Papa's drawings of the scenery. But today the news of her mother's death triggered Mama's memory and she told them this story.

"There were many refugees like us in Italy who were escaping from Hitler. All the refugee committees were overburdened with requests for visas to safe countries. Registration as an alien permitted a three-month stay. Those who weren't able to obtain visas stayed illegally, living in fear they might be deported back to Germany.

"Since refugees were not allowed to work, we spent the little money we had on renting a room. I cooked our sparse food on a one-burner gas stove, but when we ran out of money, we relied on free soup kitchens for meals.

"All we wanted was to reunite with you and get visas for all of us to find a new home, but sometimes this dream seemed hopeless. When we heard that there might be better migration possibilities in Genoa, Papa and I moved there from Milan. However, we were unable to obtain visas there either. Suddenly the political situation became very threatening. War had been threatened, but we hoped to get out of Italy before it started. Nobody knew whether Italy would side with the Nazis or the European Allies.

"We needed to get out of Italy, so we decided to go to France. We learned that people without visas were crossing the border into France at Ventimiglia about eighty miles southwest of Genoa. So, we packed our things and took a night train to that town on the Italian side of the border with France. As soon as we arrived there in the evening, we tried to get into a boat that smuggled people across the border. So many refugees were lined up, and there was no more room on the boat. The next morning, we talked to the French Consul and filed a formal application for entry. Since this meant weeks or months of waiting, we decided to walk across the border instead. We took a bus for the short trip to Grimaldi, on the Mediterranean coast.

"As we walked, I observed the beauty of the blue sky and sea, the green hills, despite my fear of what could happen. Soon there were two small buildings with a narrow strip of land between them. One station had an Italian flag, the second station flew the French flag. We were at the border. The French flag waving in the breeze seemed to say 'freedom'.

"When several soldiers came out of the French station, Papa went to talk to them. They all went inside as he tried to persuade them to let him and I enter France. I waited outside hoping and praying that this would work. Papa told me that he had almost convinced the soldiers to let them pass. But as luck would have it, who came driving up but the French Consul. When he saw Papa talking to the soldiers, he accused him of playing a double game. There was no way to cross the border today.

" We went back to Grimaldi to find other ways of crossing. It was difficult to find guides willing to help migrants cross the border as they risked being shot by French soldiers. However, some Italian government officials wanting to get rid of as many migrants as possible, expedited illegal crossings. The next day, Papa and I found an illegal crossing official in the town square surrounded by migrants. Probably bribed, he permitted everyone except the two of us to go into France without documents. He claimed that Papa was too nervous, and truthfully he had been acting very strangely during our stay in Italy.

"We decided to remain in Grimaldi, refusing to give up hope of getting into France. Two days later an order came evacuating all civilians out of Grimaldi and other border towns, so we returned to Genoa to wait for legal visas. The roads were jammed with other evacuees loaded with bundles getting away. On the train back, I felt so hopeless that I broke down and sobbed. I thought I would never see you two again, never be in a free country."

"But here we are together in the U.S." Reggie said cheerfully.

"You did it!" Steffi said. "You got out of Italy legally and into the U.S. legally."

"Is that when Papa began having problems?" Steffi asked curiously, very aware that Papa was not there with them.

"Yes," Mama said sadly. "His mental problems began soon after we left Vienna and became immigrants." She continued, "You know he really is a genius at inventing so many different things."

"And I know he loves me, even if I don't see him," Reggie said.

"Yes, Papa always wanted more than anything to be with the daughters he loves," Mama said comfortingly.

Teddy concludes: I understood that desperate people will try anything to reach their goal.

CHAPTER 10

U.S. CITIZENS AT HOME

Citizenship Thanksgiving.

Teddy observes: I listen to the new American citizens.

Real American, U.S. citizens at last! In 1946, after living here for six years the family became citizens. In May Mama received her Certificate of Naturalization. The Naturalization ceremony was brief but full of meaning as Mary Dush, age fifty and other immigrants became U.S. citizens. Mama immediately filed paperwork for her two minor daughters to become citizens.

A few days before Thanksgiving, fourteen-year-old Steffi and twelve-year-old Reggie became U.S. citizens too. Now the family could celebrate this all-American holiday with a real sense of belonging. After the Thanksgiving service at church, Mama baked a small turkey, stuffed it with rosemary-spiced breadcrumbs. They had peas and carrots, creamy mashed potatoes and an apple pie for dessert. They talked about the Pilgrims who came to America for religious freedom.

"I think the Pilgrims were immigrants like us," Steffi said.

"Now are we still immigrants or refugees?" Mama asked.

"No! We are citizens!" They all shouted.

"We have much to be thankful for this Thanksgiving." Mama said seriously.

"Let's thank God that we are American citizens now," Steffi said.

"Let's thank God that this is our country," Reggie added.

"The land of the free and the home of the brave," Steffi sang.

"Sweet land of liberty," Reggie sang.

Teddy concludes: I understood how important it is to become a citizen of the country you live in.

American girls, 1950.

Teddy observes: I have watched the transformation of shy young immigrants to confident American girls.

Now Steffi and Reggie were no longer immigrants, no longer the newcomers in school, outsiders. During their seven years in North Carolina, they had acquired a slight Southern accent – no hint of German or British English remained. As resilient young girls, they had survived the war in Austria, England and the U.S., as well as separation from their parents. They had adapted to a new language, home, schools and lifestyle .Steffi and Reggie fit in... American citizens, high school graduates ready for college. Steffie and Reggie had found home.

Teddy concludes: I understood how immigrants become Americans.

APPENDIX A: PARALLEL EVENTS, CONNECTING STORIES

Teddy's World War II immigration story to your story

	WW II Story	Your Story
First Home	house in Vienna, Austria	
New Homes	English village, Brooklyn, Cincinnati, Bat Cave & Brevard, NC	

	WW II Story	Your Story
First Language	German	
Second Language	English	

	WW II Story	Your Story
Family Separation	Children and parents	
Family Reunion	One and a half years later with their mother	

	WW II Story	Your Story
ConflictP	1939-Austria, 1940-	

Begins	England, 1941- U.S.	
Conflict Ends	World War II ends 1945	

	WW II Story	Your Story
First School	Home school, 1st-2nd grade	
New School	PS 198 Brooklyn, 3rd grade	

	WW II Story	Your Story
Immigration	1.Austria to England 2.England to U.S.	
requirements	Medical check-up, passports	

		WWII Story	Your Pal
Teddy Bear		Observes and draws conclusions about all events	

Vol. 2 AFGHAN IMMIGRATION OBSERVATIONS, 2001-2021

INTRODUCTION

Full circle. I've come full circle and now I am writing about it. The full circle connects past to present, World War II immigrants to Afghan War immigrants. It connects continents – Europe and Asia to North America. It connects cities – Vienna, Austria to Vienna, Virginia and Kabul, Afghanistan to Vienna, Virginia. I've come full circle from war to peace, from fear to freedom. I've spanned an enormous growth in technology – from analog to digital, from telegram to text, from propeller to jet, from daily news to 24/7 news flashes.

Let me re-introduce myself – my name is Teddy Bear and I was a fifth birthday gift in 1937 to Steffi Dush from her grandmother. I'm a fast learner and draw conclusions about what I observe. In other words, I quickly understand what's going on. I perceive parallels between historical events then and now.

I've come from being hauled around like a baby to having my own office from which to write. I've come full circle from observing events to compiling and writing about them. I just completed volume 1, World War II Immigration Observations - Austrian to American girls. (much to my satisfaction). Now I am ready to write this second part. That means compiling my immigration observations from Kabul to Vienna. This truly closes the circle of time... From 1937 to 2021, and includes historical parallels which I've observed over the last eighty-four years.

CHAPTER 1

TEDDY'S HALF-CENTURY

1950-2000.

My life in the cedar chest began after Steffi's high school graduation. I was in good company with a sailor doll and Reggie's Jemima Puddle Duck from England. I had been a watcher rather than close companion for years now. Sadly, I understood that teenagers don't need cuddly teddy bears in their lives.

My home in the cedar chest for fifty years (1950 to 2000) was stable and secure, even as Steffi and the chest moved from one house to another. With my extra-sensitive ears, I heard about Steffi's college years and how she became acquainted with her husband, Tim. I learned about each of the four babies as they came along. I heard Mama when she came to visit from Colorado. I paid particular attention to Reggie's voice when she and her husband and children visited. Almost every weekend, Papa told stories to his three granddaughters and grandson. I heard the childish voices deepen as they became teens and experienced dramas. I knew when each child left for college and formed new bonds. I was aware of Steffi's difficult time when she and Tim divorced. I was really grateful for my safe, comfortable in-cederation at that time.

It was wonderful to witness Steffi's joy at finding Pal, her true love, their marriage and nest building. I got to know the new stepchildren and grandchildren as they visited and became part of the family. It was heartening to realize that everyone was college educated, had careers and successfully set up a home and raised a family.

Over the years, my cedar home became a historical clothing archive. There were tiny socks, bootees, jackets, newborn hospital mementos, sleepers, bibs and bonnets. Later, ruffled play suits and Easter dresses were added, then Girl Scout-badge sashes, graduation gowns and tassels. I relished the cedar wood grain pattern, muted colors and aroma which repeled insects.

Meanwhile during this half-century, I had become an avid reader. I learned about the evolution of bears, variety and place in society throughout history. I became intimately acquainted with all fictional bears as well. I began writing and longed to become an author.

In late December 1999, I began to feel a strong urge. A new century was dawning and it was time for my life in the cedar chest to end. Kicking the lid with my paws systematically, I made a crack in the well-worn reddish wood – demanding an exodus.

A new era began on January first, 2000, when Steffi lifted the lid and carried me out with due pomp and circumstance. The constant kicking had worn the soles off my paws, so Steffi gently covered them with soft felt slippers. My new place of honor was a rocking chair on top of the closed desk in the home office. There I was a participant in Steffi and Pal's daily life. I learned a lot by watching Steffi and Pal writing and working on their computers, tablets, phones. I observed their interactions with family, friends and colleagues. Thirteen years later, I empathized with Steffi when her dear husband died. Coping with grief, she searched through old documents and photos to write his biography.

Now I am fortunate to actually see Steffi's grown children and their families. Playing a large role in the next generation immigration story is Dan, a videographer for a major TV channel.

I was happy to see Reggie and her children when they visited. She had married Mohl, originally a PhD student from Pakistan, and moved from North Carolina to Colorado. She had moved from church to mosque, from student to professor's wife. Reggie was a mother of five, a writer and an activist, helping immigrants and international students in need.

CHAPTER 2

THE AFGHAN CONNECTION

<u>Tuesday, September 11, 2001.</u>

Teddy observation: I listened and watched the horrifying events of September 11 in Vienna, Virginia.

Sixty-nine year old Steffi and seventy-four year old Pal were packing the car for a week-long trip to their favorite beach, Chincoteague on Virginia's Eastern Shore. Suddenly the telephone rang.

"Turn on the TV. We are being attacked!"

8:46 a.m. Three planes crashed into the Twin Towers of the World Trade Center in New York City. Al Qaeda terrorists had hijacked three commercial airplanes from California. Steffi and Pal watched the TV in horror as the one hundred and ten story Twin Towers burned and collapsed in a flaming inferno.

9:37 p.m. There was the sound of sirens. Terrorists had hijacked and crashed another plane into the Pentagon, U.S. military headquarters in near-by Arlington.

10:03 An airplane crashed in Shanksville, Pennsylvania. Passengers tried to gain control of the plane after a terrorist hijacked it. The terrorists did not reach their target of the White House or the Capitol.

Steffi and Pal along with all Americans would never forget September 11 – a day of horror and sorrow for the victims and praise for first responders who rescued victims. Nearly three thousand people died, on September 11, the first time the U.S. mainland had been directly attacked.

Wednesday, Sept. 12, 2001. President Bush reacts.

President George W. Bush speaks to the nation: 'The United States of America will use all our resources to conquer this enemy al-Qaeda terrorists. We will rally the world. Every nation in every region now has a decision to make. Either you are with us or you are with the terrorists."

Sept. 20,2001: President Bush declares War on Terror

President Bush's address to the nation and Congress: 'Our Tar on Terror begins with al Qaeda, but it does not end there. It will not end until every terrorist group of global reach has been found, stopped and defeated'.

October 2001: United States and Great Britain launch airstrikes at the Taliban and al Qaeda training camps and targets in Afghanistan. The ground war begins in Kandahar Province. Britain, Turkey, Germany, Italy, The Netherlands, France and Poland all send troops to Afghanistan.

Teddy conclusion: I understood that this attack had serious implications for all Americans and that this was the beginning of another war.

August 2009. Dan meets AS in Afghanistan.

Teddy's observation: I listen as Steffi's son, Dan, tells his story.
    Dan shoots videos of news events for television. He travels

to wherever something important is happening. Dan tells his Mom, Steffi, this story:

"In late August 2009, I arrived in Kabul, Afghanistan with my video camera equipment and the CBS television crew. We planned to embed with military Special Forces in Kandahar and also with the Marines in Helmand Province for four or five weeks. It was a grueling trip with temperatures reaching one hundred and fifteen degrees and constant danger from Taliban ambushes, land mines and sniper fire.

"Returning to Kabul, I first met AS at the media safe house when he escorted our TV crew to dinner. When we left the country, I remember AS seemed to know everyone at the airport and made the otherwise difficult experience very easy.

"The next year, we returned to film a story near AS' home in the Panjshir Valley. AS was our translator and driver and he proudly showed us the wreckage of Soviet tanks and helicopters his father and uncle had helped to take down in the 1980's. It was Ramadan, he and the other drivers were fasting in the intense heat and long days as we traveled from our safe house in Kabul to various locations.

"As AS and I got to know each other, I met his family, learned his family history and began to rely on him to keep us safe.

"On subsequent trips, AS would escort us to the military bases, sometimes at great personal risk. When we shopped in the markets, he would scan the crowds, and with a quick whistle tell us if it was no longer safe and time to head back to the cars. Sometimes I knew when a confrontation at a checkpoint or in a bad neighborhood was a close call, and other times I only found out later.

"As the security situation grew worse, AS' life became more

perilous as a result of working with us. He carried an AK-47 rifle and would walk with it over his shoulder as we took pictures around the city. Finally, the Taliban threatened to kill him for working with the American media. It was this death threat that brought him to the U.S. for safety.

Teddy conclusion: I learned how people develop relationships.

2001-2021. War in Afghanistan.

Teddy observation: I hear the news about another war.

After the terrorist attack on the U.S. on 9/11, war started in Afghanistan. The Taliban were in charge of the Islamic Emirate of Afghanistan. The U.S. and allies invaded Afghanistan to stop the Taliban and to keep al-Qaeda out of the country. For most of the war, the fighting was between Taliban insurgents against NATO and Afghan Armed Forces. Then on August 15, 2021, the Taliban regained power, nineteen years and eight months after defeating the Afghan Armed Forces following the withdrawal of most NATO forces.

Teddy conclusion: I understood that the U.S. is now involved in a war.

July, 2016 Steffi meets AS

Teddy observation: I listen as Steffi tells me about her introduction to AS.

Steffi greets her family in Dan and Bab's backyard. Dan and Babs' daughter, Lina, her husband Kasti and six-month old baby, Anka are visiting from Germany.

"I'm so glad to see you!" Steffi says to her granddaughter Lina, and then holds out her arms for baby Anka. As she cuddles her six-month old great-granddaughter, Steffi remembers lovingly holding her own babies and then grandchildren just like this.

Dan introduces a young man who has just arrived. "This is AS, my friend and interpreter in Afghanistan."

"Are you visiting the U.S.?" Lina asks. "I'm visiting from Germany."

"No," AS replies. "I am seeking asylum in the U.S. The Taliban says they will kill me because I worked with Americans."

"He needs to live here," Dan says, "And bring his family here where it is safe."

"Yes, I have five children," AS says. "My youngest is like your baby."

Anka, who is playing with a toy on the ground starts to fuss. AS picks her up and tenderly soothes her until she is all smiles again.

Steffi observes and says to Dan, "This is a good man."

Later Steffi has a discussion with her son. "I have lots of room in my house that I'd be glad to share with AS."

Dan says, "He needs a place to live, and since you live alone it would be good to have another person there."

"I think that Pal would approve of this decision," Steffi said. She recalled her husband working for a covert government agency. He had been instrumental in providing weapon support for the mujahedeen in the Soviet-Afghan War.

"AS' father and grandfather were mujahedeen fighting for their homeland in that war," Dan said. "I agree – Pal would want to help their grandson."

So, all the connections came together and immigrant AS

found an American home with former immigrant Steffi.

Steffi introduces AS to Reggie in Colorado by WhatsApp. She also welcomes him to the family.

Teddy's conclusion: Part two of the immigration saga begins when AS goes to live in Steffi's home in Vienna, Virginia.

AS becomes enmeshed in Steffi's family.

Teddy's observation: I listen and watch AS in Steffi's home.

Soon Steffi's other children and grandchildren get to know and like AS.

"Dan calls him 'brother'," Rena says. "So, he's our brother too."

"He's really a good guy, and helps Mom," Maddy says. "I'm glad he's here."

Steffi's family comes to appreciate AS' culinary skills as he cooks his special rice and other dishes for family dinners and celebrations. He shares dried raisins, nuts and mulberries sent from the Valley and brews healthy teas.

AS is always ready to help with whatever needs doing around the house. Dan shows him how to trim bushes, cut branches as needed and mow the lawn. Steffi no longer needs to pay for lawn service. AS takes over more and more chores around the house.

When granddaughter, Kitty visits with her young son, Dean, AS plays with him. Dean reminds him of his youngest, Ami. The grandchildren enjoy talking to AS about his experiences.

Teddy's conclusion: It is easy to become part of a family when you participate in everything.

<u>AS' Afghan childhood.</u>

Teddy's observation: I listen as AS tells Steffi about his childhood in Afghanistan.

"One of my first memories is of Soviet jets dropping bombs onto my village, Mata in the Panjshir Valley. Two families were killed, and the only survivors were two babies. I remember walking miles to the bombsite, where everyone was yelling and crying.

"I also remember my father greeting the great leader, Ahmad Shah Massoud in Khenje. A large crowd was following the leader when he greeted my father personally, but I had lost sight of my dad. When everyone quieted to listen to Massoud speak, I was very close to him. It was only later that I found my father. Being close to and hearing the Great Massoud had a great impact on my life. My family and I are Tajiks.

"Another memory is of long-range missiles, shot by the Soviet-led government from Kabul to the Valley, lighting up the sky at night. One rocket hit not far from our house. We moved to the mountain emerald mine for a week. I was seven years old and remember the four-hour walk, while my younger brother and two sisters were carried. While in the mine. I saw mujahedeen with an American stinger (shoulder-carried anti-aircraft weapon).

"I began my schooling in the first grade by walking three miles from Mata to the Khenje District School. In second grade, the other village boys and I attended school under a mulberry tree in the village center. Our teacher, a mullah, wrote on a blackboard propped against the tree. We sat on the ground in a semi-circle, copying what he wrote into our notebooks, learning to read and write Dari, do arithmetic and to read the Koran in Arabic. I remember that sometimes the teacher would ask a boy to shake the tree so that we could snack on mulberries, and we would get a drink by lapping water from the small creek nearby. When I was in third grade, my family moved to Kabul where I attended a real school. There we had our first telephone.

"By the time we returned to the village I was in fourth grade and the school had moved to a classroom in the basement of the mosque, with forty or so boys sitting on the floor copying from the board. From 1996 to 2001, I walked three miles to the Khenje District High School for seventh to twelfth grade. I didn't graduate from high school at that time because I started working. I also remember clearly the Great Massoud warning us by radio not to go to school because of a bomb threat by the Taliban. I learned much about the world from my father and the big world map and a globe that we had at home.

Teddy's conclusion: Children in other countries may have very different childhood experiences.

Aug.1, 2018. A moment in time that changed everything.

Teddy's observation: I listen as Steffi tells about a momentous event in court.

It took only seven minutes in the small Justice Department courtroom for justice to be served. Justice in this case, asylum for AS was granted quickly and easily. After filing a USCIS asylum-application two-and a-half years ago, two asylum hearings in which asylum was denied and an immigration court case scheduled for the next year, AS finally acquired asylum as fast as that a man's life changed! Now AS could request asylum for his wife and children... The family could be reunited and live unafraid in the U.S.

Teddy's conclusion: I understood the importance of receiving asylum for family reunification.

Introducing AS' family.

Teddy's observation: I get to know the children by phone.

AS (Dad) talks to his wife and children daily on WhatsApp except when they have no electricity, no way to charge their phone - no way to connect. When it's morning here, it's bedtime there, eight hour time difference. The two youngest Ami and Guls often compete about who talks to daddy, chattering in their native Dari. The older girls, Hela and Wasi politely greet Grandma (Steffi) in English "How are you?" Dad gives directions to oldest son, Naz. Then Guls proudly shows off their pet bird. Wasi tells Dad that she thought the rabbit was a robot the first time she saw the pet rabbit in its cage.

The family who live in an apartment in the capital city of Kabul will go for a brief visit to the Valley. AS grew up in the family home in the Panjshir Valley surrounded by high mountains. There is a mountain behind the house and the river nearby. Here there is freedom and clean, pure air, very different from the crowded city. Sheep and goats wander around and long-time neighbors stop by to chat... Men and boys together, women and girls in another room. AS monitors his family by phone wherever they are.

Teddy's conclusion: I understood how important it is for children to feel connected to a far-away parent.

Winter 2020. Life in Kabul, Afghanistan.

Teddy's observation: I hear about this second-hand.

Guls, Hela and Wasi's public schools are closed due to the pandemic. Six-year old Ami has never been to school. Every weekday, fifteen-year old Naz rides a school bus to a private K-12 school next to the mosque. He has math, computer science, literature and grammar, geography, history and English classes. Everyone speaks Dari and observes prayer time. Masked, boys and girls study in separate classrooms.

Dad pays a tutor to teach the girls English. She teaches them to decode, but not comprehend. Ami and Guls can sing the A-B-C song, but not recognize the letters.

Mom, Naz, Wasi, Hela, Guls and Ami are at home in their apartment in Kabul.

Hela says, "We can't go to school because of Corona virus. We have to stay at home all the time."

"But I'm glad that we can go to the madrassa class," Wasi says. "We learn new verses every day." Mother and children go to daily classes at the madrassa next to the mosque at different times. The girls wear long black dresses and dark red scarves. At madrassa they learn to read the Holy Quran (Koran) in Farsi. Girls and boys are together in a class, but sit on different sides of the room. Everyone has a madrassa card (a type of ID) allowing them to attend the class.

Inside their apartment, the family hears the sound of a car bomb exploding, screams and loud cries and people running. Ami dives under a pillow, Guls runs to Mother. Naz peeks out the window, while Hela and Wasi hide in a far corner. Everyone shelters in the middle of the house, the kitchen. It's so loud and scary. "The Taliban got through security at the American University," Mom says looking at live shots on her phone. "That's close to our house," Naz says.

"I'm scared," Guls cries. She knows that no one can predict where or when the Taliban will strike.

Mom tries to comfort her by saying, "Soon we will be with

Dad in America."

"When?" Guls asks angrily. "You keep saying soon. Dad keeps saying soon."

"Soon never comes," Ami sobs.

Note: Weekdays in Afghanistan are Saturday to Wednesday and weekends are Thursday and Friday. The family speaks their native Dari.

Teddy's conclusion: I understood once again how important it is for parents and children to keep in touch with each other when they are apart.

April 8 -May 2021. Preparing to leave home.

Teddy's observation: I hear about this second-hand.

"We have an appointment to go to the U.S. Embassy on April eighth," Mom says happily to her children. "Naz and I have to go first. Then we will all have medical exams to get U.S. visas on our passports."

On April 20, all the family go to an American clinic for medical exams and shots. A month later on 17, 2021, they get their passport visas. Now Dad books airline flights and arranges for a helper in the Dubai airport (a difficult stop to maneuver alone). No one in the family has ever been on an airplane or even been in the Kabul airport. AS and Steffi try to prepare them with information about airport and airplane procedures. Mother and the children pack large suitcases and say goodbye to their grandmother and other relatives they are leaving behind.

April 8, 2021, Vienna, Virginia.

Teddy's observation: Now 83 years later I am a participant in the immigration process once again. For four years I've been a witness, but now sitting in my rocking chair, I am on-duty as the guardian of the hard copy of AS's immigration documents I also keep a sharp eye on the computer hard drive, the Ipad and Iphone.

"They're coming!" AS announced gleefully. "Five years. I haven't been with my children for five-and-a-half years. Ami was just a baby."

With tears of joy streaming down her face, Steffi, hugs AS. "It's finally coming true and you will be together again.

AS rejoices when his wife's and oldest son's Interview with all documents at the U.S. Now Embassy is finally complete. Now the family can move on to the next steps in the immigration process – medical exams and then passport visas.

USCIS form I-485; Application to Register Permanent Residence or adjust status, AS.

USCIS form I-730 Relative Asylee Relative Petition for each family member

Steffi recalls preparing to reunite with their parents in 1940 and the long process of departure from England to the U.S. She also remembers the disappointment at not being met by Mama and Papa after one-and-a-half years. Steffi calls Reggie to tell her the good news.

Teddy's conclusion: I understood that the process of reuniting a family requires many official actions.

CHAPTER 3

TRANSITION BETWEEN HOMES

<u>May 23, 2021, Flying from Afghanistan to America.</u>

Teddy's observation: I hear about this later.

Now the family are passengers in Hamid Karzai International Airport. Masked, they wait in line to check-in. First, they must show negative corona test results along with passports and tickets.

"This suitcase is too heavy," The airline ticket agent says. "You will have to remove some items to meet the weight limit." Mom takes out some clothes and books. Each bag is too heavy, so the children have to choose and dump toys, notebooks, clothes. Ami cries when her doll can't go and everyone is sad to leave things they value.

With boarding passes, they enter an airplane for the first time and find their seats. Naz has the window seat beside Ami and Hela. In the next row, Mom sits with Guls and Wasi on the two-hour flight to Dubai. They fasten their seatbelts as they watch the fasten seat belt sign. They feel their ears pop as the plane ascends and see clouds from above. The children experiment with opening tray tables and using the TV monitor. They listen to the flight attendant and choose a drink and snack.

They experience their first descent onto the runways in Dubai. The hired helper meets the family to escort them through the large, complicated Dubai International Airport. She takes them from one terminal to another. Backpacks fall off on the escalator as they move up a level. Then in a big waiting room, the children play games, they all relax and eat.

Once on the plane to the U.S. they can see the ocean below on the monitor. The children watch cartoons and play games, trade blankets and pillows as the lights turn off for the night portion of the flight.

After many hours in the plane, everyone is excited as they prepare for landing at Dulles International Airport and finally seeing Dad again.

Teddy's conclusion: I understood that AS' family is having new experiences. Everyone looks forward to reunion.

CHAPTER 4

BIG CHANGES AT HOME IN VIENNA

<u>May 23, 2021. Reunited family</u>

Teddy observation: Having watched young Steffi and Reggie's lives change drastically because of oppression and war in Europe, I observe the new refugee family from war-torn Afghanistan adapt to a new home on a foreign continent and different culture. Sitting in my rocking chair, I write in my tablet.

*Five and a half years since wife and children last saw their father in person.
*Two years and nine months since AS was granted asylum in the U.S. and applied for asylee family reunification with his family in Afghanistan.
*Four months and three days since President Biden took office.
*One year and two months since the beginning of the Covid 19 Pandemic.

When the family arrives at the airport and exits through Customs, it is not Dad who is there to greet them. The first person they see is Dan, their old friend from Kabul. Getting their luggage, Dan guides them outside to where Dad waits by the car.

Joyful Dad greets Mom and Ami and Guls, Wasi and Hela and Naz. Together at last! AS is reunited with his wife and children after five-and a-half years. Dad drives his family home through the suburban countryside, talking happily together.

When AS' car pulls into the driveway, Grandma-Steffi welcomes the family to their new home in Vienna, Virginia.

Like Steffi and Reggie, twelve-year old Hela and thirteen-year old Wasi leave the only home they have ever known. They also depart from a capital city that is besieged by bombing. Unlike Steffi and Reggie, they do not travel alone, or leave both parents. Hela and Wasi's mother is with them, along with their two younger sisters Ami and Guls and brother Naz. They reunite with their Dad, who they haven't seen in person for five-and-a-half years. Unlike Steffi and Reggie, whose only contact was by airmail letter, they have had almost daily video phone conversations with their father.

Both sets of immigrants leave grandmothers behind in their native countries. Both leave their countries at a crucial time as war and war-like conditions accelerate soon after. Like Steffi and Reggie, Hela and Wasi have to become acquainted with their new home. Unlike Steffi and Reggie, they had seen all parts of the house and yard virtually. They do, however have to adapt to a different culture and lifestyle, which Steffi and Reggie did not. Both sets of children have very limited English, so everything has to be named. While Steffi and Reggie moved from a German-speaking to an English-speaking environment, Hela and Wasi don't experience total immersion since everyone else in the family speaks their native Dari. Just as Steffi and Reggie quickly bonded with Aunt Alice and Dora, Wasi and Hela bond with Steffi who they call Grandma. No dog, but lots of birds and squirrels and the Brood-X cicadas which abound at this time.

Steffi writes thank you letters: "Humbly grateful for the compassion, kindness, expertise, generosity and support of a team without whom this family would never have been reunited – the Biden administration, senators and congressmen, pro-bono attorneys, dedicated friends.

The goodness of all these individuals and the completion of

the immigration process serve to reinforce my belief that the United States does indeed live up to its creed emblazoned on the Statue of Liberty, "Give me your tired, your poor, your huddled masses yearning to breathe free." The very same words that I beheld on my arrival in New York harbor as a World War II refugee eighty-one years ago."

Note: Steffi appreciates Vice-President Harris' response to this when it arrives later.

Teddy's conclusion: Everyone has to adapt to a new situation when a family reunites in a new home.

First days in the new home.

Teddy's observation: Sitting in my rocking chair, I observe the present, remember the past and write.

Soon in Kabul became now in Vienna. Now the children are with their father, the wife is with her husband in their new home. Lots of hugs and kisses, jabbering away – happiness. Dad shows his family all around the house and they tour the yard. He shows them the bird feeders and birdbath, introduces them to birds, squirrels and a chipmunk. Ami and Guls happily hold Dad's hands as they walk around. The children naturally play on the swings in the back yard. Dad shows them their rooms downstairs and their bunk beds. In the living room, they try playing all the musical instruments – piano, ukulele, tambourine, flute, drum, mandolin and the harp.

Steffi and Reggie sat outside in the garden having English tea with Aunt Alice and Dora. Now Hela and Wasi sit outside under the blue umbrella, at the patio table having American grilled hamburgers with the whole family. Steffi and Reggie walked around the neighborhood with Dora, while Wasi and Hela and the siblings walk to the playground with Dad, though he drives them everywhere else. Dora and Aunt Alice's neighbors were kind to the little refugees in their village. Steffi-Grandma's neighbors bring smiles and welcome gifts to new refugees on their street.

Both sets of children experience being near a river. Steffi and Reggie walked along the gently flowing Broads River, while Hela and Wasi view the Potomac River as it rages over Great Falls.

A Memorial Day picnic in the neighbor's back yard, introduces Wasi, Hela, Naz, Guls and Amian to hot dogs, lemonade and watermelon. Learning to toast marshmallows over a fire to make 'some mores' is an all-American treat. In the evening, Grandma guides the family into putting colored stripes and stars together to make their own American flag as they talk about the red, white and blue.

Teddy's conclusion: Children quickly learn about their new environment.

Enmeshed in family, June 2021.

Teddy's observation: I watch how Steffi's whole family embraces the new family.

Connected families in 2021:

AS family: wife; Bea, children; Naz, Wasi, Hela, Guls, and Ami.

Steffi's family: four children and their spouses, four step-children and their spouses, ten grandchildren, five step-grandchildren, three great-grandchildren, five step-great-grandchildren

Reggie's family – husband, five children, eighteen grandchildren, eighteen great-grandchildren

In preparation for AS family's arrival, Steffi's children and grandchildren all pitched in. They'd brought bunk beds, blankets and towels, equipping the downstairs as living space for a family of seven. They all got to know each other in small groups outside under the blue umbrella because of the Pandemic. Maggie and her daughters, Lil and Sil bring cookies and play with the children. Ginny, her daughter Kay and grandson Dare bring fruit snacks and balls to toss in the back yard.

AS introduced his family to Reggie and her family in Colorado by phone. Reggie welcomed the new immigrants at her sister's home. Reggie's son and his wife sent backpacks and water bottles to the children for school.

Teddy's conclusion. Two families can quickly become enmeshed with each other.

Dad's daily homecoming.

Teddy observation: Sitting in my rocking chair, I observe, remember and write.

Dad commutes to work, in Washington DC, daily and his return home in the evening is always a happy reunion. The girls all rush to hug him and bask in his presence as he listens to everyone. Grandma watches empathetically and writes a poem.

Greeted by joyous hugs
Dad returns from work
to his long-awaited family.
Rapturous reunion
with Dad daily
after his work

and children & Mom's lessons
outside in the fresh air
in the peaceful neighborhood
freedom!

Teddy's conclusion: Daily after-work reunions are happy occasions.

<u>English immersion.</u>

Teddy's observation: Sitting in my rocking chair, I observe, remember and write

Every morning Aunt Alice sat with Steffi teaching her to read easy books in English and to write simple sentences. She taught Reggie the alphabet, while Dora worked on counting and math facts. They all sang nursery rhymes and Aunt Alice read them fairy tales with lots of pictures. They read labels on boxes and bags, signs and street names in the village.

The large dining room table becomes the classroom for formal lessons. Teacher-Grandma tries to have daily lessons at ten a.m. for Hela, Wasi and Naz. The two younger children will have their lessons later.

"Get out your notebook and pencil," Grandma says. She holds up the calendar and points to today's date. They repeat the date and practice the days of the week.

Grandma spells and writes 'Today is Tuesday.' on the white board. "Open your notebook to a new page and write the sentence."

"Good job!" Teacher-Grandma says as she looks at each child's writing. Then she hands out a simple story about the birds, squirrels and chipmunks they watched yesterday, Wasi, Hela and Naz take turns reading the text and recalling their experience.

They talk about the questions and Teacher models, writing the answer. Homework is to reread the story and highlight the animals.

The children learn to listen, speak, read and write English through their everyday experiences.

Teddy's conclusion: Children acquire English through immersion as well as direct instruction.

<u>June 2021. New experiences.</u>

Teddy observation: I have interesting experiences with seventeen-year brood x cicadas which are in full concert by mid-June.

In the afternoon Mom, Ami, Guls and Grandma sit outside under the blue umbrella. Guls and Ami have a pan of sticky sand and mold sandcastles on the table. The ground, trees and bushes are covered with cicada shells and cicadas. Some cicadas try to the climb table and chair legs.

Grandma says, "Look, the cicada is on my finger."

Ami holds out her finger and the cicada moves over. She laughs at the tickly feeling when it moves. Then Guls picks up a cicada from the ground. "Cicada," she says looking into its red eyes. Suddenly she has a brilliant idea and puts the cicada on top of a sandcastle. "Cicada house," she says.

Ami makes a door in the house for her cicada. "Cicada house."

When a cicada suddenly flies up, Mom shakes it away. "It's okay," Grandma says, "Some people don't like cicadas."

"I like," Ami says looking at her cicada.

"Look at its beautiful wings," Grandma says and points to a wing. "So beautiful." Ami and Guls nod their heads. "Listen!"

Grandma says cupping her ears and looking up. They all hear the loud cicada concert of many males singing together to attract females. "The cicadas are singing."

Teddy's conclusion: The family has the opportunity to learn about a rare natural phenomenon.

<u>Multipurpose rainbow colors.</u>

Teddy's observation: Sitting in my rocking chair, I observe how rainbow colors can make connections.

The family sits around the table as Grandma teaches a lesson on colors. Pointing to the rainbow picture, they name the colors, "Red, orange, yellow, green, blue, purple."

Grandma points to the red. "What color is this?"

"Red."

"R-e-d, red" Hela spells.

"Very good!" Grandma says.

"Red is color," Wasi says pointing to R in the alphabet. "R is rainbow."

"Very good!" Grandma says.

Today's lesson is on rainbow fruit - Rainbow fruit math. On the table: a red plate with twelve cherries and five red apples, an orange plate with six tangerines and three peaches, a yellow plate with four bananas and three lemons, a green plate with seven limes and two green pears, a blue plate with twelve blueberries, a purple plate with six plums and thirteen purple grapes.

After the children name all the fruit and colors, Grandma says, "Now let's do some math." She hands Hela the plate of cherries. "How many cherries?"

Hela counts the cherries one by one, "Twelve!" she shouts.

"Yea!" Grandma cheers and writes '<u>red</u>' on the white board and then she writes 12.

"Now count the apples," Grandma says. "How many red apples?"

"Five!"

"Yea!" Grandma cheers and writes +5 on the white board. 12 + 5 = __ "If there are 12 red cherries and 5 red apples. How many red fruits all together?"

Wasi counts in Dari and answers, "Seventy".

"Seventeen?" Grandma writes 17.

"Yes, seventeen."

As a teacher, Grandma knows how difficult it is to hear and pronounce the difference between the two similar numbers, seventeen and seventy.

By using real fruit and later vegetables, Steffi the Grandma-teacher is working up to My Plate and a healthy diet. Grandma passes out a rainbow-fruit math worksheet that she wrote and printed. She guides them through each problem reading, calculating the answer and writing the answers. Teaching the rainbow colors and "Brown Bear – what do you see?" prove to be versatile bases for extending concepts and vocabulary for everyone.

Steffi remembers her first formal introduction to mimeographed worksheets in third grade in Brooklyn, her experiences in making copies as a teacher and now the ease of using your own computer and printer.

Teddy's conclusion: Some simple objects have multiple uses.

<u>July 5.2021 Amin Independence Day.</u>

Teddy's observation: Sitting in my rocking chair, I observe everything, remember and write.

July 5, 2021 is the day the immigration story comes full

circle for Steffi. It begins with leaving Vienna, Austria because of Nazi occupation in 1939 to arriving in the U.S and residing there for eighty-two years. It continues the immigration circle with AS and finally his whole family leaving Taliban-controlled Afghanistan and coming to the U.S, to Vienna, VA – home!

After more than five years, the Amin family is free, all together at Uncle Dan and Aunt Bab's house with Anka and her Mom and Dad, Grandma free to swim in the pool, play games, eat a picnic supper, play with sparklers in the yard. Free to be together!

Yesterday the family celebrated their first Fourth of July. They attended a neighborhood picnic, waved American flags and watched the fireworks on the Mall in D.C.

Young voices shriek gleefully As children swing carefree. Peace and tranquility. A secure environment fully free. A simple symbol is a backyard swing; swingers dream of achieving anything. Higher and higher, back and forth; rhythmic movement itself is strength. Great gratitude for Dan's impunity in creating this golden opportunity.

Teddy's conclusion: First and second immigration stories come full circle.

CHAPTER 5

A LONG WAR ENDS

War.

Teddy's observation: I remember each declaration of war that Steffi and Reggie experienced.

March 12, 1938. Anschluss.

"Hitler, the Fűhrer , will now give an address about the Anschluss to the Austrian people."

Sept. 3, 1939 Britain at war.

Prime Minister Neville Chamberlin explains that Britain is declaring war against Germany.

Dec. 8, 1941. War begins in America.

President Roosevelt (FDR) speaking to Congress and the American people. "Yesterday, December 7, 1941 — a date which will live in infamy…"

Aug. 15, 1945. The Japanese officially surrender to the Allies. World War II ends.

August 16, 2021. The war in Afghanistan ends.

Teddy's observation: I watch the family react to breaking news from Afghanistan on Dad's cell phone, TV news and the newspaper.

The Washington Post headlines – AFGHANISTAN FALLS TO

TALIBAN.

Taliban fighters took control of Kabul and authority over all of Afghanistan as the western-backed government collapsed.

"The Taliban have captured another province," AS says despairingly as he watches the grim images on his phone.

Naz and Hela and Wasi, Guls and Ami watch too and listen to their parents talk. They've known the Taliban as bad men all their lives. Steffi recall her own childhood visions of the bad guys, the Nazis. First the Nazis and now the Taliban, a recurring nightmare – control by ruthless leaders using deadly weapons.

Over the summer, despite negotiations with the U.S. government, Taliban have taken control of more and more provinces and in eleven days controlled the government in the capital.

August 31, 2021. Americans exit from Afghanistan.

AMERICA EXITS AFGHANISTAN.
Last plane leaves, but efforts to help people depart will continue.

The U.S. ended its longest war in history, and its twenty-year presence in Afghanistan, as the last U.S. aircraft took off from Kabul Airport at one minute before midnight on August the 31, carrying the remaining American troops and diplomats.

Teddy's conclusion: I understood that this long war was finally over.

First Days of School in the U.S.

Teddy's observation: I watch and listen as the children talk about school with Grandma.

On the first day of the 2021-22 school year, five immigrant children enter Fairfax County Public Schools (FCPS) with backpacks full of school supplies including masks and water bottles.

-Exactly 3 months after the family's arrival in Vienna, Virginia from Kabul, Afghanistan.
-Amidst constant visual news of the Taliban takeover, parents' anxiety about relatives, actually meeting with a refugee mother and son and a cousin air-lifted out of Kabul.
-Amidst the surge of Covid-19's Delta variant.

New experiences:

-Monday to Friday weekday schedules and weekends off.
    -Boys and girls together in classrooms.
    -Kindergarten Ami and fourth grade Guls attend a large elementary school with many classrooms, halls, cafeteria, gym, offices; instruction in English.
    -Seventh and eighth grade middle schoolers, Hela and Wasi and ninth grade high-schooler, Naz have ESOL classes and block scheduling on large school campuses.
    -No textbooks, all instructional materials online.
    -A choice of food to eat in the cafeteria (check the lunch menu to eliminate non-Halal meat items).
    -Elementary, middle and high school students receive FCPS planners and are issued school laptops to take home.
    -Middle schoolers and high schoolers walk to the bus stop and ride the school bus to and from school.

Teddy's conclusion: I understood that public schools in Virginia are very different from their previous school experiences.

CHAPTER 6

GIVING THANKS

The first Thanksgiving in America – 1621 2021.

Teddy's observation: I watch as the family learns about Thanksgiving in preparation for the feast.

Preparation for Thanksgiving.

The family learns about the Pilgrims and the Wampanoags and the first Thanksgiving. Grandma reads and they discuss illustrated Thanksgiving books. A table holds a miniature scenario with Pilgrim and Native American dolls, corn and pumpkins, apple trees and a forest with deer, foxes and turkeys. The girls string together colorful leaves to represent a forest and hang up a fall forest backdrop. A small Mayflower picture rests on the Atlantic Ocean on the globe. Realia brings the past to life.

Each day Grandma talks with the family about thankfulness. "What are you thankful for today?" The lists include – coming here, being together, my teacher, holiday and macaroni.

Interestingly when Steffi views the Pilgrims as immigrants rather than settlers, she sees similarities with AS' family and current Afghan immigrants.

An immigrant is a person who comes to a country to live there.

• In 1620, the Pilgrims were immigrants from England seeking religious freedom.

In 2021, Afghan immigrants seek political freedom – freedom from the Taliban. Immigrants move to a country which has freedom of speech, religion, the press and to protest.

• The English King gave the Pilgrims permission to settle on land in America. The land, however belonged to the native people, not the king. The Pilgrims worked hard to cut trees and build houses in an unfamiliar land. They made an English colony.

Today immigrants live with another family or rent an apartment or house. They have to work for years to be able to buy property.

• Pilgrim immigrants from England had to adapt to a totally new environment.

Afghan immigrants have to adapt to a new environment.

• The Pilgrims did not know how to obtain food. Native Americans helped the Pilgrims learn how to hunt, use natural resources, grow and store crops.

American agencies, individuals and organizations assist/mentor new immigrants in obtaining housing, food, jobs, medical insurance, schools, etc.

• The Pilgrims learned to grow, cook and eat new food – corn, squash and pumpkins.

New immigrants learn to buy and eat typically American food – hamburgers, hot dogs, pizza, chips, apple pie, ice cream. Muslims learn which foods are Halal and which are not.

• In the fall of 1621, the Pilgrims harvested their crops, picked fruit and nuts, stored food to eat in the winter.

In the fall of 2021, new immigrants get winter clothing - jackets, gloves, and boots. Family and friends all help to provide the new family with winter gear.

Writing in English, each person in the family expresses his/her thankfulness.

AS during his fourth Thanksgiving, but his first with his family said:" I thank God for every moment that we are breathing and worship God together. Before supper and after every prayer we thank God for having another family and friends here in the U.S.A, especially having the kind of angels in our life. Wethank and pray to God for justice and peace for human beings."

Mom and Naz during their first Thanksgiving say: "I thank God for uniting us after six years, that we are together. I thank God for having Grandma in our life, I am thankful to God for our family and for everything one thousand times."

Wasi and Hela say: "I am grateful for all family together, coming here."

Guls says: "I am thankful to God for family and coming here and school and animals, food."

Ami says: "I am thankful for family, Grandma, Dad, Mom, teacher, Uncle Dan, Anka, and Aunty Lina."

Teddy's conclusion: The family understands the true meaning of Thanksgiving.

The Thanksgiving feast, 2021

Teddy's observation: I watch as two families blend together on Thanksgiving Day.

Two long tables await the guests in Uncle Dan and Aunt Babs' house. The smells, the festive setting is traditional Thanksgiving. Covered dishes await on a side table as the cooks finish up in the kitchen. So much thought and work have gone into this special meal. Chefs Dan and Jon, Lina and Bab, and Maggie - each has his/her specialty. Five-year old Anka made name cards so each person knows where to sit. When all is ready and everyone is seated, Grandma offers a prayer of thankfulness and a toast to togetherness. Then dishes are passed around and everyone relishes the turkey (which is Halal) and stuffing, mashed potatoes, cranberry relish, green beans and sweet potatoes, corn pudding and rolls. Desserts – pumpkin pie and apple pie and pumpkin cheesecake follow a break. Thankful for togetherness. Thankful for food preparation. Thankful for the well-set tables. Thankful for the stalwart cooks. Thankful for traditional feast. Thankful for the first Thanksgiving. For new immigrants here living

After the feast.

Aunt Lina organizes a dance contest for after-turkey exercise. The family poses for a first Thanksgiving portrait as all chant "pumpkin pie". Quiet time – all the children from five to fifteen huddle on the floor as Lina teaches them to play the card game Uno. Everyone is sated with good food and loving kindness.

Two families united in thankfulness and peace. One former immigrant's family connecting with the new immigrant family. The American immigration cycle continues as the new immigrant family finds a home in the U.S.

Teddy's conclusion: On this day of thankfulness, two families thankfully close the circle together.

APPENDIX A:

LESSONS FOR IMMIGRANTS

Immigrants' experiences	How do you feel?
Immigrants may be frightened by real threats and anxious about the future.	
Young immigrants separated from their parents need to feel cared for and secure.	
It is vital for separated parents and children to keep in touch with each other.	
Children are resilient, adapting to changing situations and life-styles.	
Children acquire a second language easily, while it is more difficult for adults.	
Transitions between homes may be difficult.	
It takes time, teamwork, and much official action to reunite a family who are in different countries.	
Children want to be like their peers.	
When young immigrants become permanent residents and citizens of their adopted country, they feel at	

home. Older immigrants may long for their home country.	
Successful immigrants are resilient, adaptable, feel safe, secure and at home, look toward to the future, not stuck in the past.	
Everyone has to make adaptations when there is a war or conflict. War or conflict imposes constraints on everyone.	
People have a feeling of relief, when a long war or conflict is finally over.	
Finding humor in a situation helps to dispel fear, anxiety and sadness.	
When adult immigrants live in a new country, aside from laws, they can choose which customs they want to maintain and which they are willing to change.	
Young immigrants who come to a new country without their parents, adapt differently than those who are accompanied.	

Addendum: In August 2022, AS and his family are even more thankful as his mother, siblings and cousins arrive and find a new, safe home in the U.S.

APPENDIX B:

PARALLEL EVENTS, CONNECTING STORIES

Teddy's World War II story to Afghan immigration story to your story

	WWII Story	Afghan Story	Your Story
First Home	Vienna, Austria house.	Kabul apartment & Panjsher Valley house, Afghanistan.	
New Homes	English village, Brooklyn, Cincinnati, Bat Cave & Brevard, NC.	Vienna, VA.	

	WWII Story	Afghan Story	Your Story
First Language	German	Dari	
Second Language	English	English	

	WWII Story	Afghan Story	Your Story
Family Separation	Children and parents.	Wife & children from father.	
Family Reunion	Children reunite with mother after one and a half years.	Wife & children reunite with father after five and a half years.	

	WWII Story	Afghan Story	Your Story
Conflict Begins	Austria -1939; England -1940; U.S. – 1941.	Sept. 11, 2001 (9/11) - War on Terror begins.	
Conflict Ends	World War II ends 1945.	Aug. 31, 2021 Afghan War ends.	

	WWII Story	Afghan Story	Your Story
First School	Home school, first –2nd grade.	Private & public schools.	
New School	P.S. 198 Brooklyn, 3rd grade.	Fairfax County Public Schools, elementary, middle, high schools.	

	WWII Story	Afghan Story	Your Story
Immigration	Austria to England. England to U.S.	Afghanistan to U.S.	
Requirements	Medical check-up, passports.	Passport visas, immunizations, Covid tests.	

APPENDIX C:

IMMIGRANTS ADAPT TO A NEW ENVIRONMENT

	Austria to England	England to U.S.	Afghanistan to U.S.
Family	Parents & children to parent substitutes.	1)Parent substitutes, 2) institution, 3) reunite with one parent.	Mother & children reunite with father.
Place	City suburb (Vienna) to English village.	big city (NY), city (Cincinnati), mountain village (Bat Cave, NC).	Capital city (Kabul) to Washington, DC suburb (Vienna, VA).
Language	German to Immersion in English -English literacy, love of reading.	American English	Dari to English Left to right, front to back reading/writing
Daily life	Care for dog chickens, garden.	Life in big city	Weekdays- Mon. – Fri.routines, jeans/T-shirts, shoes in house, bunk beds.
School	Home school to	Gr. three	Public schools.

	home school.	public school in big city.	
Customs	Church on Sunday.	Church/Sunday School on Sunday	five prayer times daily.
Holidays	Christmas same.	Christmas same New - July 4, Thanksgiving	New - July 4, Halloween, Thanksgiving, Christmas.
Conflict	Nazis- bombing to air raids, restrictions, rationing.	Rationing.	Taliban - car bombs, shooting, explosions, fighting.
Requirements			Seat belts, traffic signals, Immunizations

APPENDIX D.

HISTORY REPEATS ITSELF

HISTORY REPEATS – MASKS

September 1939. Gas masks required.
When Nazi bombing begins in Great Britain, gas masks are required as part of air raid protection. Everyone is fitted with a gas mask.

March 2020. Masks required in public.
The World Health Organization (WHO) declares a world-wide pandemic of the corona virus disease COVID-19. U.S. Center for Disease Control (CDC) issues guidelines to slow the spread: Wear a mask to protect yourself and others, social distancing from those not in your family, frequent hand-washing, quarantine if exposed, isolate if sick.

HISTORY REPEATS – HEALTH

1941.
The sign outside the infirmary door read: Warning measles. This section of the infirmary was in quarantine because of a measles epidemic at the Children's Home. Children who were infected by the highly contagious virus were quarantined here for at least fourteen days.

2020-21 Covid-19 quarantine for fourteen days after contracting or exposure to the virus.

HISTORY REPEATS – DISCRIMINATION

March 12, 1938.
Hitler, the Führergives a speech to the Austrian people about the Anschluss, the political union of Austria and Germany. The new Nazi government claims that people are not equal, that Jews or people with Jewish heritage don't have any rights.

April 10, 1938.
On April tenth Austrians voted in a plebiscite to determine whether they are for or against the Anschluss – to be part of Germany's Third Reich ruled by Hitler and his Nazi Party. The next day's newspapers announced that 98% of Austrians voted to approve Anschluss. However, the voting was rigged, it was not a correct count of people's ballots. Austrians did not want to be part of Germany, but their votes were changed

Nov. 9, 1938.
Kristallnacht. Nazi looters broke shop windows, stole goods from stores, set fires to destroy Jewish-owned stores and businesses. The police did nothing. The Nazis wanted to take money and property away from Jews and send them out of the country.

Jan. 20, 2016 – Jan. 20, 2021.
President Donald Trump calls to 'make America great again', but is against immigration and protecting the environment. President Trump's anti-immigrant administration builds a wall along the U.S. Mexican border, issues travel bans from specific countries, promotes ICE raids, separates parents and children at the

Mexican border, encourages white supremacists, rescinds environmental protections.

Jan. 6, 2021. Encouraged by President Trump, a mob breaks glass windows and enters the Capitol of the U.S. with little initial resistance by police. The rioters violently vandalize the Capitol, attempting to overturn valid election results. Rioters are subsequently caught, tried and sentenced to jail terms.

HISTORY REPEATS – WAR

World War II

March 13, 1938. Hitler starts war.
Anschluss. Austria is annexed to Nazi Germany under dictator, Hitler

Britain enters war, Sept. 3, 1939
Prime Minister Neville Chamberlin declares war against Germany.

U.S. enters war, Dec. 8, 1941
President Franklin Delano Roosevelt (FDR) declares war.

May 9, 1945. V-E Day, Victory in Europe Day.
Germany surrenders to the Allies.

Aug. 15, 1945.
The Japanese surrender to the Allies. World War II ends.

War on Terror in Afghanistan and Iraq begins after the September

11, 2001 terrorist attack.
President George W. Bush announces a comprehensive plan to seek out and stop terrorists around the world.

August 16, 2021. Afghanistan falls.
Taliban fighters take control of Kabul and all of Afghanistan. The western-backed government collapses.

August 31, 2021. *AMERICA EXITS AFGHANISTAN.*
The U.S. ends its longest war in history after twenty years.